The Glitches

The Glitch

The Empties

The Norm

This is a work of fiction. Names, characters, places and incidents either are the product of imagination or are used fictitiously. Any resemblance to actual persons, living or dead, events or locales, is entirely coincidental.

RELAY PUBLISHING EDITION, APRIL 20178

Cover Art by Rebecca Frank Art

www.relaypub.com

THE GLITCH

The Glitches Series
Book One

Ramona Finn

Blurb

On the brink of extinction, being human means more than just surviving.

In Lib's world, it's dangerous to deviate from the norm. In fact, for someone who doesn't live up to the Artificial Intelligence's standards, it's practically a death sentence. Lib learns this the hard way when she wakes up in a barren wasteland, with her memories erased, and only one thought lodged in her mind:

"It's all my fault."

Lib is a Glitch—an imperfect human component of the utopian world called the Norm. Now she's thrown out, Lib will be forced to team up with another Glitch, Raj, and the mysterious Rogue Wolf and his clan to survive. Wolf only cares about the survival of his group, but Raj thinks they can hack the A.I. and change the Norm for the better.

Now, Lib will have to decide which path to choose—whether to go with striking loner Raj or stay with Wolf and his tight-knit group. Her heart is drawn to both, but she's carrying a deadly secret that could jeopardize them all. Will she be able to save her newfound family and stop the A.I. before it's too late?

Sign up to Ramona Finn's mailing list to be notified of new releases and get exclusive excerpts!

Sign Up at

www.ramonafinn.com/newsletter

You can also find me on Facebook!

www.facebook.com/ramonafinnbooks

Table of Contents

Chapter One

A screech tears through the air and wakes me. The sound echoes and feels almost an echo of the noise in my head. Someone is screaming.

Scrambling to my feet sets my head spinning. I stagger on shaky legs. My stomach gives a heave, and I almost fall to the cracked ground. I want to laugh—I'm as cracked as the ground. I stagger and then walk. Then I run. I don't know where I'm going except toward that scream—toward the other voice. The world around me seems wrong—it's all bright and brown. To one side of me, a wall towers into the sky, impossibly tall, dull and gray, leaving me wanting to beat on it with my fists. The screaming is getting louder. I'm close.

The need to get there fast beats in me, pumping blood and burning in my lungs. Rocks trip my bare feet, cutting sharp and hot, leaving me limping, skipping. Ignore it—the words come easy to mind, but I'm stumbling like I haven't used my legs in a long, long time. But something else pops up as well—it's all my fault.

I don't know why those thoughts come to me. But I do know I've reached the sound of whoever else is in trouble. In front of me is a building—but what is that really? It is round—a semi-circle, with one end open and a railing and what looks like a wide-viewing screen. The flashing green of the lights seems out of place in this dry world.

Just like me.

The thought leaves my head aching, but I have no time for that. The building has a metal platform. A girl is slumped there. Her screams have gone to whimpers now. She looks younger than me, small and fragile. She has one hand on the railing in front of her. The lights glow and sparks jump out, so white they dazzle. The air stinks as if something is burning. I fear the something is the girl's skin on the hand that seems stuck to the metal railing.

Moving forward, I put my hands next to the girl's on the railing. I'm moving on instinct, not thought. I don't know why, but words leap into my head without my asking—motherboard… electronic connection…access to mainframe AI. My stomach gives another sickening lurch. I'm shaking all over. I know what to do—and I don't know why I know this.

I plant one hand on the railing next to the girl's.

Connection: Secure.

Tiny pinpricks jab my palm. A dozen of them. Connections spark within me—I can feel the power slip over my skin and into my mind. With a blink, everything in the dry, brown world around me is no longer anything I can see. Instead, I'm not standing inside a room, dark and blue that is soothing in a way the other dry, dusty place was not. Next to me, the girl stands, her image wavering—and I know we are here in this other place, but we are not really here.

This is the artificial world—it is a construct I see with my mind. But the question comes up—how do I know this? A certainty swells in my chest. I do know this place—it is where I am from. But…that makes no sense to me. How can I be from an artificial world—a computer construct?

Glancing around me, I search for answers—and for a way to save this girl.

A round, black machine sits on her back. Its black arms and legs make it look like it is meant to simulate a small person. But it has no face. No skin. Firewall. The word pops into my head.

Reaching out, I ghost a touch over the plate on the firewall's chest. Power tingles on my fingertips, but I don't know if that is coming from me or the firewall. I do know it is attacking the girl—it is a security measure and the girl triggered it. But I don't like that it's hurting her.

I find a button and press it—something clicks and code appears, scrolling over the black surface of the firewall's body. A thousand tiny messages appear in binary—ones and zeros. It's clumsy code. Why do I know that? Unease shivers through me, but in the other world—the dry and dusty one—I can still hear the girl's whimpers. Turning to the firewall, I pick out the lines of code that will end this. With a touch, the lines are wiped out.

We can go now, so I put a hand on the girl's wrists and think those words to her.

The world snaps and breaks. For an instant, everything seems to be blackness. The soothing room of blue and cool vanishes—but then I stand again on the metal platform. I no longer hold the railing, but the girl is with me. She is no longer screaming. She glances at me, parts her lips as if to say something, but then slumps down to sprawl on the platform.

Nonfunctional.

Unconscious.

The two words leave me frowning—which is it? I changed the code to make the firewall nonfunctional. Did that in turn leave the girl unconscious—nonfunctional?

It's all my fault.

Is it my fault this girl is hurt? I don't know.

Frowning, I rub at the ache deep in the center of my chest. That's new. I don't know if it's good or not. I also don't know how I got out here in this dry and brown world. Glancing around, it seems to me that even the sky is a pale color—almost blue but not quite. It is so different from the cool, blue room—the artificial place—that it frightens me. I want to go back, but if I do will the firewalls attack me?

Reaching up, I put cold fingers to my cheeks. They are wet and I don't know why, but the wetness is leaking from my eyes. My throat now seems too tight, too dry. What happened to me that I am in the big, open, frightening place?

Maybe the girl will know.

Squatting down next to her, I touch her arm and shake her shoulder. She moves but only when I push her.

"Why can't I remember?" The words come out rough and my voice sounds as if I have not used it in a long time. The girl doesn't answer.

Sitting down next to her, I decide she is longer than I am. Taller—that's the word. But her face is darker than mine. My skin shows pale white and angry red as if it has been burned. Her skin is not as smooth as mine. Tiny golden hairs cover her arms. Those hairs match the bright ones on her head, but that hair is pulled up and back and I don't know why. I lean closer. Do I know her? Her face seems angled and sharp. Her eyes are closed but the lashes look feathery soft. I sit back and tug my hair around so I can see it.

Dark, dark brown and thick. It is much shorter than that of the nonfunctional girl.

And that is because…?

No answer swims up to me from within my mind. Closing my hands into fists, I stare down at them. Did someone wipe my code clean? But…no. I am a person not a firewall—not a machine within an artificial construct. I should have memories—I know this. I pound one fist into metal and that leaves my hand sore. That's a good thing—that means this world is real.

It's all my fault.

With a frustrated growl, I sit back on my heels until my back rests against the metal wall. A rock presses into my butt. I'm tired. I want to close my eyes and wake remembering. I want the girl to wake because maybe she can tell me something. I hope she can.

"Who are you?" The words come out of my mouth mumbled. I have to wet my lips and try again. "Who am I?"

Glitch.

The word appears in my head like someone said it. I glance around us. There is no one here but the nonfunctional girl and me. It seems I'm not very functional either—which leaves me dysfunctional. I almost let out a laugh, but I don't know why that word is funny.

Lifting a hand, I open and close my fingers. I let out a breath. I know I'm alive. And in a barren world that seems to be empty except for the girl with me, this platform—which is no longer glowing or sparking—and the wall and the sun burning over us.

I am a glitch? That word feels wrong—the firewall was glitching, wasn't it when it attacked the girl? Firewalls should guard—they're not supposed to attack those who enter. Just as I knew how to shut down the firewall and free the girl from its hold, I know this. And I don't know why I do. The knowledge sits in my stomach like I've swallowed a rock.

I must find the Glitches.

The thought is like the other fragments lying around in my head—out of order, lost in mist, and has no contest for why I must do this. But it's something.

Find the Glitches.

I don't know what it means. Glancing around, I want to be back in the cool room. I touch the railing. Nothing happens. It seems to have become even more nonfunctional than the girl. I let out a whoosh of air. If I can get one tiny piece of myself back, I should be able to get more. Right now, I have no thought for what my name is, or how I know about the artificial world, but I seem to know nothing about this this outside world.

Memory…error.

It's all my fault.

“Find the Glitches,” I say to the dry, dusty air and to the girl. Maybe the Glitches will know why it’s my fault. And is that a bad thing or a good one?

The girl moves—just a flutter of her pale lashes, a flicker of a finger moving in the dust. My heart seems to skip a beat. Eagerness floods me along with the chill of fear, and I lean close and ask her, “Do you know who I am?”

Chapter Two

Moving closer, I kneel at the girl's side. I want her to wake. I want her to move and speak and tell me how this brown, dusty world works. It is getting even dustier. A wind sweeps up, pushing dirt into the air. The girl gives a groan.

Pale lashes flutter and her lids open. Her eyes startle me—they are so blue they seem a reflection of the sky. I look up just to make sure, but in the end, I decide they're not an exact match to the blue shade of the sky.

When I look back to her, those blue eyes widen. Her nostrils flare and her skin seems to pale. She tries to scrabble backward, but she can't move very well and only just sits up and stares at me.

I put out a hand, but I don't touch her. She looks as if she might become nonfunctional again if I do.

Glancing at my hand, she wets her lips. That reminds me I'm thirsty, too, but there is nothing here. No water, no food…just this girl and me. I don't want to leave here. I need to know what this girl can tell me about who I am.

"You're…functional now?" I ask.

As soon as the words are out of my mouth, she jerks away from me. That's difficult given that I'm kneeling so close and she's lying on the floor. But she manages it by using her legs to shove herself, digging her heels into the dust and pushing against cracks in the platform.

I stare at her and ask, "What are you doing?"

When her back hits the metal wall and the railing—which I now know is some kind of connector—she freezes. She glances up at the railing and then looks at me again. "You!" Her voice is high like a squeak almost.

Hope flutters in my breast. This is where she'll tell me who I am.

Her next words rush out with a breath. "You're the crazy girl who saved me."

Disappointment pulls at my shoulders and I slump back. I don't know what my expression must look like, but my lower lip quivers. I don't even know what my face looks like. I don't think it looks like this girl's, but maybe I'm wrong. Maybe we're copies. Maybe all faces look like hers.

"Why am I crazy?" I ask.

She scoots away from the railing and waves up at it. "You could have died. So could I. The hack went bad and I didn't see the sentinel until it was too late." The girl sees something in my expression that tells her I don't understand what she's saying. Her lips tug down again—she has a wide mouth. She sits up and puts her elbows on her knees. “You did save me? Yes?”

I think about her question. About the connection to the artificial construct, the room, and the firewall. It was a virtual trap. It wasn’t real. But she had connected her mind to that construct world and it was out to end her connect which would have stopped her heart with an electrical surge fed back into her body through the railing. Even as fragmented as I am, I know that much. So I nod. “Yes, I did.”

Her mouth shifts up to a sudden grin. She pops up, onto her feet like it’s the easiest thing in the world. Like she’s very strong and not recovering from being nonfunctional. Has she done this before? Reaching out a hand, she offers it to me palm up, still grinning. “I’m Skye.”

I stare at her hand and then look at her sky-eyes again.

On some level, I understand this hand-to-hand offer is a traditional greeting from…well, I don’t know from where. I should take her hand with mine, but I find myself not wanting to. If I do, I will have to tell her a name. That is the custom. I don’t have one to offer.

She waggles her hand at me. “Well?”

Slowly, I stand and brush at the dust on the gray cloth that covers me. Skye has better clothes—she has boots and cloth that covers her legs and arms as well as her chest and her hips. The cloth on her fits snug, while my cloth hangs loose as if it's not even mine. Crossing my arms makes them burn, but I keep them that way and ask, "Well, what?"

She rolls her eyes, and for a second, I wonder if she's going nonfunctional again, but it seems to only be a gesture. Hands flopping out, she asks, "Are you going to tell me your name?"

Should I make one up? Something fitting? None for no memory? My stomach knots. I don't want to lie—that is no way to connect with the only person in the world I know right now.

Letting my hands drop to the side, I say, "I can't remember."

She tilts her head to the side. Her long, tied-back hair falls forward over one shoulder. "What happened? Have you been walking around for sixteen years like this?"

I blink once. "Sixteen?" I glance down at my hands. These are young hands? "Am I sixteen? I don't know."

She takes one step closer. Her mouth pulls down and her hands tighten into fists. "You got thrown out?" She waves at the wall behind us.

I glance at the wall. It is so tall I cannot see a top, only that it curves up and seems to disappear into the sky. Turning back to her, I shake my head. The wind picks up and tugs at my hair. I reach up to brush at it, and for an instant, I know it should be longer. Who cut my hair?

"I don't…I can't remember."

She nods. "It happens that way sometimes." She waves at the wall again. "You've been tossed out. Sounds like a wipe, too. Or maybe you're out because you got an accidental wipe. That's what happened."

"How do you know all this?"

Skye shrugs. "I got thrown out, too. And you learn out here—or you die."

"Die?"

"You become nonfunctional—permanently."

I shiver. "That can happen? I thought nonfunctional—I thought it was only temporary."

She nods. Her eyes seem to turn an even darker blue, and I have to ask, "What color are my eyes?" Suddenly, it's so important. I want a mirror so I can see exactly what I look like. I will know this one small thing about myself so at least I can say one thing with certainty.

"Uh," Skye pauses and wets her lips again. "Well, they're sort of grayish. Like your jumpsuit. Or like smoke."

Reaching out, she touches the cloth I wear. A jumpsuit, she said. She smiles at me and lifts and drops one shoulder. I could reach out and hug her. She's given me a few small pieces of myself—I have gray eyes, I am sixteen.

Skye steps closer and quickly adds, "It's a really pretty color. I mean, you're pretty. Cute."

Her cheeks flood red. She frowns, chews her lower lip again, and says, "You're a Glitch. I mean, you'd know if you were a Rogue, and you're obviously not a Tech, not anymore at least, or not as far as I can tell. You being a Glitch explains the wipe."

All those words sound familiar, but I'm having difficulty parsing them. Struggling with them, images pop into my mind—flashing past so fast I can barely catch them. Tech—someone who maintains…maintains what? That part is missing. But a Glitch is a Tech who has been thrown out. But what is a Rogue?

An image appears of people, the faces blurred, but I know they're eager to be near each other, eager to hold hands, they walk along the sidewalk, heads tilted close.

The images snap off as if something cut them off.

I'm back on the platform with the wind getting stronger, in a dusty world, and Skye seems to have been speaking for some time. "—'cause they're the only ones who get kicked out."

I blink at her. "What?"

"Glitches." She says the word slowly as though I might be dumb. Maybe I am. "No one wants to keep a Glitch around."

She looks away from me. She has lean muscles that stretch the cloth she wears. Her wide mouth pulls down and I think I see something on her face that makes me think she's sad or upset about something.

I frown, and then I realize what must be the truth. "You're a Glitch, too, then?"

She nods, shrugs again and shakes her head. "Not anymore."

The way she says the words—with a sharp bite like a slap—tells me that being a Glitch is not good. I think on her words—no one wants to keep a Glitch around. Was I left here because no one wants me?

A feeling like a tear inside my chest inches upward. It cuts deeply and I start to shake inside, but more fragments sweep up at the break inside—this time they aren't images but sounds.

In my mind I hear a cool voice speaking. You are the most important thing. My greatest accomplishment. My Lib.

Lib.

The word echoes in my head and connects to something else. To my mother. My mother spoke those words to me—she said I was the most important thing. She called me Lib. Mother wanted me. I know this with a certainty, the same way I knew how to shut down the firewall. But where is Mother now? What's happened to her?

Skye's hand on my arm shakes me back to the moment. She is staring at me, the look in her eyes uncertain, almost concerned. A weight has eased, lifted from my chest. I have two more solid bits of information to cling to—I have a memory of Mother talking to me and I have a name.

"Lib." Pushing back my shoulders, I repeat the name. "Lib."

Skye's blonde eyebrows raise high on her lean face. "What's Lib?"

I smile widely at her, maybe even foolishly, but I don't care. "It's me. My name. I remember."

The girl gives me a funny look. "That's something." Skye stares at me a moment longer, as though deciding something in her own mind, but she gives a short nod and drops her hand away from me. "Lib it is. At least I don't have to call you Memory-lost-strange-girl."

She winks at me and smiles. I don't smile back, but I say, because I think it's the right response, "Yes, a mouthful."

Skye looks away from me, her gaze going up and to the sun and shadows. She frowns and her voice goes softer. "It's late. The sun is going down and the wind's coming up. We should move.

I've wasted a lot of time, and if we don't hurry, they'll move on without us."

"They?" A shiver rushes through me. I think of the memory—people holding hands and walking. Will Skye take me to those people—are they the ones she speaks of? "Who are they? Will they be okay with a…a Glitch? Do they have more Glitches?"

She looks at me and her mouth twists up at one side. "The clan. Rogues. Don't know how they'll feel about you but being out alone is not the kind of thing you wanna do. So, c'mon. Let's get a move on. They at least won't turn you out at night."

Skye turns and walks away from the wall and platform. For a moment, my feet seem stuck. I glance back at the wall. It is the only thing that is familiar to me. I don't want to leave it. What if Mother is behind it and looking for me? Should I stay and wait for her?

But what if that memory is old and Mother isn't—isn't functional?

My throat tightens. The thought is unbearable. I need Mother to be alive. I need to stay alive. I need to find the other Glitches. I glance down at my bare feet. I have nothing on them the way Skye does. But I start to walk and follow her steps.

We've only taken a dozen or so steps away from the wall before we've escaped the long shadow now cast by the wall. I wish we didn't have to leave here because, even with the sun lower in the sky, it beats down on my already hot skin.

Moisture pops up and trickles down my face. My tongue is thick and dry. I try to lick my lips, but they are dry and taste metallic. Swallowing, I glance at Skye and ask, "Is there water nearby? Anything liquid?"

Skye looks over at me, her eyes wide. "Look around you. You see any water?"

I do as she asks. Around us is brittle, cracking ground. It is as hot as my skin. The wall behind us is stark. The platform beside it had nothing other than the railing—the connect. I keep looking.

In the distance I can see the land go up. Mountains. The word pops up and I try for more memories.

Ruins.

Yes, the smaller, square bits of black and brown are pieces of what once was here. A city? Metal shoots up from the dry ground and twists like it is frozen in agony. Red dust floats and mixes with the sand over the ruins. An image flashes in my mind—green of trees, the ground covered with more green, and…it flashes off again.

All I see now are the mountains in the far distance, distorted by waves of heat. There is no water here. And I know that without it, we will die.

I glance at Skye. She's staring ahead calmly, walking with a long, firm stride. This world doesn't scare her like it does me. She jabs her thumb over her shoulder, back to where we came from. "That's what I was doing back there. Trying to hack some water. The stupid AI caught me before I could get access to open up the watcr storage."

I frown. AI? Hack?

My hands tingle as if I havc them on the board again. I wish I was back in that cool room. It seemed much more comfortable than…than here.

Skye lets out a long breath and mutters, "Wolf is going to be really disappointed."

I want to ask what's a wolf, but images of a massive animal with four legs and huge paws and fangs and golden eyes that glint pops into my mind. I ask instead, "There are wolves out here?"

Skye blinks at me. "What?"

"Wolves," I repeat, glancing behind us now, the skin prickling along my neck and down my shoulders. "You said wolf would be disappointed."

She stares at me a moment longer and breaks into a laugh. It takes her a moment to get herself under control. Irritation sparks in me. She thinks my fear is funny? Wiping tears from her eyes, she tells me, "Not wolves, Wolf. Wolf Tracker. He's a boy. Well, man. Whatever. You'll meet him when we get there."

I frown at her, glancing over my shoulder once again. The wall is growing smaller, but it is still so big. It is the only thing that seems solid in this world.

Will Mother come looking for me?

Thinking of that, I want to tell Skye I have to go back.

But Skye glances at me and says, "Wolf's a Rogue. A lot of them don't like Glitches, but Wolf makes law. If he finds you useful, he'll take you in. But we need to be back by dark. That's law. We break law, we're out. And it's hard to find other Rogue clans that'll take Glitches."

Find the Glitches.

The words echo in me almost like someone said them. The drive to complete this task is so strong it frightens me a little. But I must do it. The lingering desire to stay can't stand against the need pushing at me. It is stronger than my thirst. It is stronger than anything else and beats inside me like the heat from the sun. I must go with Skye. I must find the Glitches.

But if I am a Glitch why do I need to find them? And what will happen after that?

Chapter Three

Wolf turns out to be tall. Taller than both me and Skye by a lot. His shoulders branch out, broad and thick, encased in a dark cloth that maybe is black or maybe is just really dark and looks black because of the dim lighting. His arms are large, shaped by ropes of thick muscle. His waist dips and then his legs are the same as his arms, thick with muscles, which are only just hinted at beneath tanned cloth that doesn't look like cloth but more like soft skin. It's only when I've made it down to the tall black boots he wears on his feet that I jerk my stare back up to the top of him to find his face.

A face that is surprisingly young.

His muscles and size make him seem older, larger, but softness still lingers in his face. Enough to tell me he is barely older than me.

Or barely older than Skye seems to think I am.

"Who's this?" His deep voice washes over me in a wave that could be comforting, could be menacing. It is still too early to tell.

"Lib. Glitch just tossed. Found her outside the Norm."

"Skye led me across the stinking, blazing hot sand. She said this is one of the better places. Places where you can still grow some things and where you can find shade and water." The more I talk, the more Wolf's mouth pulls down. I brush at the dirt on the cloth that covers me—the jumpsuit, Skye called it. I'm dirty, tired, hungry, thirsty, and starting to not like Wolf. He's looking at me as if I'm trash to dump. I'm a Glitch. And I'm not like Skye.

I tear my eyes away from Wolf and glance at Skye. She stands beside him now. She's smiling, but she shifts on her feet and reaches up with one hand to tug her hair forward over one shoulder.

Wolf's lips tug down even more. I realize with a start that he doesn't like me and I'm surprised to find this disappoints me. A lot. I'm not sure why; he's not important.

"A-are you a Glitch?" I ask with a stutter.

His voice turns unfriendly, and he looks straight at Skye. "You should have left her."

"The way you left me? Wolf, she can be useful. She helped me with the hack." Skye spreads her hands wide.

"Helped enough to get water access?"

Skye drops her head low and stares at the ground. We stand in a hole—well, we came into this through a hole, but this place is both cool and warm. The walls seem smooth—someone made this place. Light flickers, which is odd, and I don't understand how the light can jump as it does. It comes from a spot on the ground instead of from above, and the air smells of smoke, but it is not a bad smell. Not like a circuit burning.

That thought leaves me frowning, but before I can trace it back to where it came from, Wolf folds his arms across his broad chest, causing the muscles to stand out. "You know law, Skye. You brought a stranger into the clan."

Skye looks up, her blue eyes going bright. "Where else will she go? She's a Glitch and wiped, too. She saved my life—I know law about that, too. That makes her clan."

His gaze flickers to me and then back to Skye. "Wiped? You sure?"

Skye shrugs. "She couldn't even remember her name at first. I know wiped when I see it."

Wolf glances at me. I want to tell him he can keep his laws and clans and I will go, but Skye's warning that no one should be alone at night echoes in me. Skye calls it Outside—says all Outside is bad, or most of it. Rogues know how to live Outside—they use the Glitches sometimes to access the Norm and get water. And I have to find the Glitches.

Skye continues to stare up at Wolf, her lower lip pushed out now. Her eyes seem bigger and the blue in them shines in the flickering light from the ground. Wolf stares her down for a long moment, but eventually he gives a short nod. He looks at me. His eyes are darker than the world above right now.

"Law is law. For saving Skye's life, you can share the fire." He waves at the light on the ground. He turns and stalks down into the darkness, away from us—and from the fire.

Skye turns to me, grinning.

With a glance at her, I walk after Wolf. My skin is hot again and my breaths fast. My strides carry me quickly into the darkness that is not so dark. I catch sight of Wolf's broad back. Behind me, Skye calls, "Lib, where are you going?

Before I can touch Wolf, he stops and turns so fast I almost run into him.

Licking my dry lips, I ask, "Why are you angry with Skye?"

When he speaks, it's like a wolf growl. His white teeth gleam against his darker skin. "You don't know law. That's bad. It's worse if you can't remember. How do I judge if you're a threat to my clan?"

I can feel my face pulling together in a frown. His logic is good. Smart. I don't even know what I am. But I don't feel the urge to hurt anyone. I'm too small to do much.

I shake my head. "But you take in Glitches—?"

He makes a frustrated noise, and says, “Some Glitches. Most can’t be trusted. They’re unstable—more than Skye even.”

I don’t know why his words sting, but they do. I flinch and turn away, but he puts a hand on my arm and stops me. “You come out from the Norm and think you’re better because you’ve seen paradise. But you were tossed out. Techs decided you’re broken—and you are. You can’t live in the Outside without clan, but you still think Rogues aren’t even people, don’t you?”

His dark eyes flash. He’s so angry that I can feel heat burning off him, brighter and hotter than the sun. I want to step back and away. He seems to grow in size until he takes up all the space, all the air, all the world. He moves closer. I will not back down. Heart thudding, I crane my neck back so I can see his face.

The words are out of my mouth before I can think if they are wise. “Then why help any Glitches?”

There is a long pause. It seems as if I can feel his heart beating, too, through his skin where his hand touches my arm. I drag in a breath and wait.

A short minute later, he yells, “Bear!” The word echoes. I want to clap my hands over my ears, but Wolf still holds me. Quieter, he says, “I am Wolf Tracker, leader of Tracker Clan, and it is up to me to make law and keep law. Law says we keep what is useful. Law says we waste nothing. Law says you earned the right to sit by the fire by helping the clan.”

Before I can do more than take in a harsh breath, another boy appears out of the darkness. He, too, is big. White lines crisscross his skin. His arms are bare. His cloth covers only his chest, his waist, his legs and not his arms. I don't know why he has lines on him—they looked like old tears that have mended. He doesn't seem to take up the whole room like Wolf does, but he frowns at me and I don't want to be near him. Like Wolf, he has dark hair and eyes.

Wolf pushes me toward the boy, who must be Bear. "Take her to the Coffin. No one sees her without my say."

Bear nods and grabs me by the wrist. He drags me away. I stumble along after, too tired to do more than that. If I can find a place to fall down, that will be enough. I need to be nonfunctional for a time.

But on my back, I feel Wolf's stare, hot as the sun.

* * *

The Coffin turns out to be a box in a ditch. It smells like wet animals and stale mold. The ditch looks hollowed out by hand. Dirt and straw line the inside. Beneath that is metal of some kind, half rusted just like the walls, which are taller than I am. I can stand straight, but I'd rather lie down. The top is open with bars across it. They don't look rusted. Bear slings some kind of nearly transparent material over the bars. From under the cloth, I can see shadows that move but no details.

I am a prisoner. But I'm too tired to care.

Bear comes back to pull away the cloth and hand down a hunk of something that smells good. It's charred and tough, but I eat what I can. Bear also leaves a small jug of stone with sweet, cold water. I drink it all, and my eyes keep drifting closed. When Bear leaves, I lie down and wiggle a little to get as comfortable as I can in the dirt and straw.

I know Wolf put me here because he doesn't trust me. I don't know why that bothers me like it does.

Eyes closing, I try not to think. It's not comfortable here, but it's not uncomfortable either. The straw itches, but I am warm. In fact, I could be nonfunctional anywhere right now.

My mind starts to drift. That's when I hear a woman say my name.

Lib.

Has Skye come to help me? But the voice sounds wrong. The voice isn't really here. I know that, but I don't know how I know.

Lib, this is important. Do you understand?

Suddenly, I am not in this hole anymore. I'm back in that cool, blue room. I know this place…don't I? I know it from more than just having been here during the connect.

Differences are bad. They are destructive. Humanity embraced them, praised them. As a result, humanity failed. If not for me, the human race would not even be a memory.

Her voice is soothing…and so familiar in a way that nothing else could ever be. She cares for me. She is my everything.

This is why Glitches must be cast out.

I flinch because that word applies to me now. A worming dissatisfaction crawls under my skin. But I am an important Glitch. I am necessary. Aren't I?

You understand why you must go.

I don't understand! I want to shout the words. I want to bunch a fist and yell and hit something. With a shout, I sit up.

It's dark…I am still in the hole. That Coffin. I am alone—and even the memory of her voice is fading. But was it a memory or something else? A wish?

I am no closer to knowing the answer than I am to knowing who I am, but now my shoulders slump with the burden of sadness. It claws at me like something trying to tear me apart from the inside. The woman—the one speaking in my head—is important to me. Is she Mother? Or someone else?

All I know it that she cast me out.

Lying down again, I shiver. I am truly alone.

Chapter Four

At some point I go nonfunctional again. I know because now I jerk into function sweating, my heart pumping and my breaths fast and shallow. Voices echo, but it is difficult to judge if they are close or a long way away.

"...just throw us in lock up!" I don't recognize this voice, but it is deep and smooth. It is also male. And angry.

Someone makes a derisive sound, a snort of some kind. A second later I realize that might be Wolf because he answers, "Long as you live with clan, you listen to law. Law says I must do what is good for the whole clan."

Sitting up, I wonder if I could climb the walls so I can peek through the material covering. Just moving leaves me aching. I don't know how long I've been nonfunctional, but I am thirsty again. My stomach growls. I slump back against the cool, hard wall and just listen.

"And what is good? Good is throwing her away? Good is wasting a life? That's not law. If she was a Rogue from any other clan, you'd have welcomed her." Whoever is talking sounds angry. I am a little surprised he is challenging Wolf.

Wolf sounds angry, too. I can picture his dark eyes flashing as he growls out the word, "Yeah. That's 'cause I can trust another clan. I protect my people."

"So do I."

I frown. Why is this other male thinking I need his protection? Or that I am his kind?

The voices fade, and then I hear Wolf say, "Look, I get it. But I can't risk it. She's a liability."

"Liability?" The first voice goes high on the question. "She's a Glitch, like me or Skye. She's also just a girl."

Putting my hands on my knees, I stiffen at this. I may be a Glitch but I don't need anyone else to defend me. I could do that. Still, I am grateful that someone is speaking up for me, even if I would rather do it myself.

Wolf's voice suddenly jumps louder. "Why doesn't she remember anything? You ever hear of a wipe doing that?"

"So what? We all come out of the Norm messed up. Skye was like that."

"No," Wolf answered, his voice low and firm. "Skye was out of it, and then she seized. When she came to, she remembered who she was and why she'd been tossed."

"Wolf, I know law, too. You make sure we all know it. Law says you need a reason to keep her shut in. What's the reason? You just don't like her face?"

"Watch yourself. Never mistakc who is in charge. Never."

"Law says that. Law also says you can call council and that's what I'm asking for now."

I wait to hear more, but the voices have moved away. I strain to hear more, but the conversation is dcfinitcly ovcr. I wish Bcar would at least bring me more water.

* * *

Nonfunctional seems to have some function. I close my eyes, but images come—maybe they're memories. In my mind, I hear the woman again. I can almost see her face, too, but when I come to full function all I have is a vague, misty image that fades too fast for me to hold. I'm left with sensing the same thing I knew before—she is important to me, but she is not here.

Overhead, the metal bars groan and slide back.

Frowning, I look up. Light makes me squint and my heart beats faster. I hadn't heard anyone coming.

Scrambling to my feet, I press my lips tight. I don't want to ruin my chance to get out of here. Maybe it's Bear with food and water. Or maybe it's Wolf come to throw me out. Or Skye?

The bars and cloth move away and a girl—younger than me—peers down at me. She is not someone I recognize.

Her cheeks are chubby and her smile takes up half her round face. The effect makes her look very young—maybe twelve or so. Her nose is wide and flat, like a large button, and her black eyebrows are heavy. Her hair looks wild and bright ribbons of pink, greens and blues are tangled into the frizzy black.

The girl leans down. Ribbons flutter on the cloth she wears, which is tan like Wolf's pants. She grins at me, her teeth whiter against her dark skin.

"Are you going to come up or what?" she asks. Her voice is deeper and now she seems older than I thought at first.

I glance around. I'm not sure I can pull myself up and out. With a shrug, I tell her, "I'd like to, but—" I wave at the metal walls as if that will tell her everything.

The girl rolls her eyes. She braces her hands on her knees. "Well, then come up already."

"I can't jump that high and I don't have wings. And why are you saving me?"

The girl laughs. "Saving. I like that."

Her laugh sparks something inside—a sharp flush of embarrassment. The feeling is pointless, but I can't help it. She doesn't have to laugh at me.

"Sorry." She says the word but it doesn't sound like an apology. She's still giggling. Turning away, she comes back and tosses down a flexible ladder. The word rope pops into mind.

I eye it for a moment. This doesn't seem much better than climbing metal walls, but I grab one of the rungs and put a foot on another. The rope holds. And what's the point in being surly and staying stuck down here?

When I get to the top, I scramble over the lip of the Coffin and roll onto my feet. They hurt. My skin still burns a little, but I ignore it.

The girl has her head tipped to one side and faces me. "I'm Bird Sees Far."

I blink at her. "Is that a name or a function?"

She smiles, lifts one shoulder and waves a hand as if that is an answer. "You're Lib. Wolf should have told me sooner that you'd come."

Irritation with her itches on my skin. Doesn't she ever answer any question? I try a statement instead. "That's an…unusual name."

She folds her arms across her chest which is small enough that it is nearly nonexistent. She is definitely young. "Glitches always think Rogue names are odd, but who goes by Lib?"

I frown and a sense of uneasiness slips down my back like a trickle of cold water. "How did you know my name? Did Wolf tell you?"

Bird Sees Far looks away from me off to the side. "You're the new Glitch. I overheard Skye say your name."

It is a good answer, a valid one, but I still think she's lying about that. I don't know why and I don't have a reason to push for the truth. "Lib is a perfectly good name. And it's all I have."

She gives a nod as if I just gave the right answer. "It's better than a Tech number. Did you choose it or did the AI give it to you?"

"What's an AI?"

She glances at me sideways now. "That's right—you don't remember. Well, you should learn that we're named by our clan. I'm from the Sees Far clan, but I came to stay with the Trackers. Our names give us a spirit animal that represents our true selves." She grins again. "I fly like a bird."

I can't help staring at her. I don't understand most of what she is saying. "What's a bird? And…well, what's an AI? And a Tech?"

Her grin fades. "You know more than you think. But don't worry." She starts walking away. She is taking the light with her—it's a small fire she holds on a stick. I'm torn between following her and just climbing back into where I was. It was safe there. And warm. But I can't go back.

I have to find the Glitches.

I start walking after her. She's surprisingly fast for such a small girl.

Bird Sees Far glances back. "I'll take you to the healer. He can fix up your feet so you'll be ready."

"Ready for what?"

She doesn't answer. I hurry to catch up with her but step on a rock. With a wince, I stumble along, my skin even hotter now. "I'm getting frustrated at being ignored." I mutter the words, and Bird Sees Far must hear, but she doesn't glance back this time. Even if she did let me out, I am not sure I like her.

"Just what are Rogues?" I ask mostly to see if she'll ignore this question, too, but I'm curious. The light is bright enough for me to see the walls are stone and marked with designs. They all look the same to me.

Bird Sees Far glances back again, her dark eyebrows pulled tight. "You know more than you think you do."

I narrow my eyes at her. But she faces forward, her steps long, and then says, "I don't know why we're called Rogues—we just are. Anyone born Outside the Norm is born to one of the Rogue clans. The Norm—that's that big wall where you came from. Remember?" She glances back at me, her eyes bright.

I make a noise, but something surfaces in my mind. "It's a biosphere. The Techs…the Techs have to maintain it."

"See, you do know. Anyway, when a Tech goes bad, goes wrong, the damaged ones become Glitches. Like you." Her voice is bright as she says this.

I flinch. I don't want to be damaged and I don't like the idea that I was thrown away. This would mean Mother isn't looking for me—she wouldn't want me back. I can't bring myself to say this. I don't want Bird Sees Far to know what I feel. And I want her to keep talking. Her words jog memories loose from me. I am greedy for more, so I ask, "How many Rogue clans are there?"

"Oh, I don't know. We're pretty scattered. Larger clans bring danger, so we keep small and ready to move if we must. We have to watch for drones."

I think back now to how Skye kept looking up the whole time we walked here. I don't know what a drone is but it must be something that comes from the sky.

"Different clans have different law. But we also share some things. We're all Outsiders. We're all human."

I study the back of Bird Sees Far's head—the wild curls and multi-colored ribbons that flash in the light from the stick she carries. I don't like the way she said that word—human. It is as if it means something different to her than it does to me. Like I am something different.

"What do you mean by that?" The words come out sharp.

Bird Sees Far doesn't answer me. We round the next curve and the tunnel opens into a wide room. I have to stop and stare. The room is tall and circular with several tunnels leading off of it. The walls are brightly painted with reds and oranges and some blues. I see shapes and the words leap into mind—wolf, bear, bird, horse, dog, cat…so many images. The paintings cover the walls as far up as I can reach and they make the room seem to come alive.

At the very center of the room, a beam of light shines down. Looking up, I can see a hole far above me. The hole is perfectly round and at the bottom is a circle of polished, black rocks and something that gives off smoke.

Several people, dressed in tattered cloth all stop what they are doing and stare at Bird and me. I don't see any blonde hair—they all have dark hair and dark eyes and closed-off faces. Skye isn't here. And no one looks friendly.

Bird taps my arm with one hand. "This way. The healer shouldn't be too busy right now." She heads across the huge room.

I hurry to catch up with her. The looks others track me with leave my skin prickling. Catching up to Bird Sees Far, I ask, "What's a healer?"

"His name is Croc, and he's good at what he does, despite the name." She grins at me like she is sharing a joke. I'm not seeing what's funny.

Bird turns to go down another tunnel, but a low, gruff voice stops us with one growled word. "Bird?"

Turning, I see Wolf. His mouth is pulled down and he doesn't look happy. Just like before, he stops near us. He is so much taller that I have to look up to see his face, but I am not going to let him just bully me. I stand my ground.

Bird Sees Far stops and turns to face Wolf. Her mouth tugs down in a small frown, but she gives a shrug with one lifted and dropped shoulder. "I'm taking her to Croc." She keeps her voice casual as if this is no big deal. I slop a hip to one side and put a hand on it. If Wolf wants to make trouble, he's going to have to work for it.

Wolf's stare strays to me. I meet that stare, and he turns away to look at Bird again. "Who said you should?"

"Did someone have to say? Her feet hurt. So does her skin. She needs care."

Wolf's stare shifts to me again. Heat rushes through me, but I stare back. This time I look away to stare at the dirt floor and the coverings on Wolf's feet—I wish I had those. Wolf mutters something harsh and then says, "Fine. Croc, then back."

"Back? Why? I think that's a little unnecessary, don't you?"

I glance at Bird. Why is she defending me? Why did she let me out? I keep my mouth shut in the hopes she can convince Wolf to let me stay out. I'll never find the other Glitches in that Coffin.

Wolf says nothing, but tension seems to hunch his broad shoulders. His eyes narrow. For a moment, he only stares at me and then at Bird.

She huffs out a breath and says, "Lib's going to be important." She says this as if she is stating a fact. I can't think why she would say this or why Wolf would believe her.

But he stands very still, staring at Bird, and I think maybe there is a kind of communication between them I can't understand.

"You saw her?"

"I did. I didn't know it was her until she got here, but now I'm sure." Bird grins.

Wolf turns his dark eyes back onto me. It seems to me as if he is really looking at me for the first time. His eyebrows are pulled together, but I'm not sensing anger from him. No…it's more like…curiosity.

He gives a nod and starts to turn away, but he glances back at Bird. "Next time, clear it with me first." Before Bird can say anything, Wolf stalks off.

There's so much I don't understand. I turn to Bird, but she's already heading down the next tunnel. "Come on. Croc's waiting.

I follow—but if Bird won't answer my questions, I'm going to have to find a way to ask Wolf. That idea leaves my stomach churning.

* * *

The healer, Croc, has a room that seems nicer than anything else I've seen. The walls have shelves filled with glass bottles and sweet-smelling plants hang from them. Something to lie on stands against the far wall—Croc is lying there when we step in but he gets up quickly.

He looks older than anyone else I have met. He is not as tall as Wolf, but he has lines on his face and his dark hair is thin and moving back from his forehead as if he is losing it. He is thin and grumbles a lot, and he takes one look at my feet and curses. "How did you let them get so bad? No, don't tell me. I never like what anyone gives me for bad excuses. Sit down, girl. Sit down."

Glancing around, I see a stool and a table. I sit on the stool. It is rough but sturdy. "My name is Lib."

"Fine. Now let's educate you about taking better care of yourself. Starting with feet first."

Croc's voice is rough, but his hands are soft and gentle as he rubs something soft and moist on my feet and then wraps cloth around them. The dull throb fades. And it smells good, too, like…the memory of the smell fades, but I know I have smelled it before. Green flashes in front of me—a plant? I am not sure. But I am incredibly grateful.

Another woman comes in with a small person—a baby—who is crying. Croc tells Bird that's all for now and waves us away so he can turn to the woman and her child. Bird leads me back to the main room. I see a flash of Skye's pale hair and relief floods me—a friend at last.

I head for where Skye sits. She looks up and spots me. With a gasp, she stands and runs to me. "Lib!" Her voice squeaks. She throws an arm around my neck. It is a strange sensation to be touched like that. "Sorry Wolf threw you into the Coffin. He's been grumpy."

I give her a shaky smile. "It's okay." I point over my shoulder. "Bird got me out." I turn, but Bird isn't there anymore. She seems to have wandered off, leaving me with Skye. I glance over at the boy who was sitting with Skye. He is standing now.

He wears cloth that is more like Skye's. It's worn and faded, but he looks different from Wolf and the others, even though his skin and hair are dark like theirs. He shakes his head and says, "Bird…is different. But if she got you out, it's probably okay."

I glance from the boy to Skye. "Why is that?"

Skye pulls me down to sit next to her and the boy sits with us. "Everyone's pretty sure Wolf will take Bird as his mate. She's going to be leading the clan with him."

My throat tightens and my shoulders knot. I can't seem to move, though I'm not entirely sure why. I don't much care for Bird—so maybe she and Wolf deserve each other. But, this still seems wrong to me. At least Bird got me out when Wolf would have left me there—maybe forever.

Looking past Skye, I stare at the boy sitting with us. His dark hair is short and curls around his face. He skin is very dark…so are his eyes. He is smiling at me in a way that leaves my skin hot again.

Skye glances at him and nudges his side with an elbow. "This is Raj."

I know he's tall from when he was standing, but he seems thin. His body is almost lost in his loose-fitting cloth, but I can see hints of lean, wiry muscle.

He's staring at me intently. "You're Lib?" His voice is soft. I recognize it immediately. He was the male arguing with Wolf. He's a Glitch. Are these two the other Glitches I was supposed to find? If they are, why doesn't this feel like success—like I have done what I need to do?

"Raj is a Glitch," Skye says, stating the obvious. "There aren't that many of us. Only two others."

I nod. This is why it doesn't feel as if I've done what I must. These are only some of the Glitches.

"A lot of Rogues don't like us," Raj mutters.

"I'm starting to understand that." I glance around the large room. When I do, stares shift away. Some of the Rogues turn away.

"People fear what is different," Raj says.

That reminds me of the memory I had—was it a memory?—in the Coffin. Different is bad. I jerk my stare back to him. "Isn't that why we're here, though? Because we're different? We're broken and that's bad."

He smiles. The expression softens his face. For a moment, he looks younger. His cheeks seem less lean. He looks…good. Although I don't think that's the right word. "Guess we're just the wrong kind of different." His gaze seems to sharpen and he asks, "What's wrong with you?"

I look away and at the bowl of food sitting between him and Skye. I don't feel hungry, but I have to do something. I hate that I don't know what is wrong with me. It makes me feel as if it must be terrible.

"Don't be a waste of flesh," Skye hisses at Raj. She swats his upper arm. "She just got here. Her getting trashed was rough, but she dumped me from a bad connect."

He straightens and looks at me, speculation bright in his dark eyes. Maybe he is thinking of apologizing. Before he can, others drift into the room. They come in from every tunnel, some chatting and laughing, some walk in silent, some come in by themselves and some come with others. I count twenty in total in the room.

The Rogues head to the stones and the spill of light from the hole in the high ceiling. One of the Rogues—an older, thin man—kneels beside the stones and knocks what sounds like two rocks together. A spark flashes. Light kindles and grows in size. I can smell burning—but it's a good smell, not like when wires are shorting.

And how do I know that?

Before I can catch the memory, it is gone. The room fills, but I notice that the Rogues seem to avoid Skye and Raj and me. Only two others—a boy with hair as pale and bright as Skye's and a girl who is very thin and small—join us. Other Glitches? I can't tell without asking. But Wolf steps out from the other Rogues. My stare goes to him. He is so much taller than anyone else. It seems impossible to look at anyone else when he is in the room. He fills up the space not just with his size but with his personality.

Everyone else quiets, and Wolf's deep voice echoes in the big cavern. "Clan and clan guests." His stare sweeps over those gathered but seems to settle on me. It doesn't stay. He looks away and I am left feeling strangely heated and bare.

"We survive another day because we work as clan. We follow law. Without the clan, the one cannot survive. Without clan, we are nothing but shades. You are mine and I am yours. That is the law."

The other Rogues echo his last words.

For a moment, something like a power surge washes through me. Do others feel this? There is no question in my mind why Wolf is the leader—his voice and his words command. I want to follow him, too. For the first time, I want to stay.

Wolf steps away, and the Rogues break into smaller groups. Wolf joins one of these groups and Bird is there, her ribbons flashing and bright. My mouth dries. I am not part of this. I am not welcome here.

I look away, glancing over at the other two Glitches, who talk quietly together. I get the impression they aren't interested in making friends the way Skye is or the way Raj might be.

Skye jumps up and waves at me to stay put. She heads toward where the Rogues seem to be gathering.

"Where's she going?" I glance at Raj.

He flashes a brief smile. "To grab food. She'll bring something back for all of us. One in each group does it like that."

Glancing back, I see he's right. One person from each small group—they sit in small groups of no more than five—has gotten up and gone over to where Skye stands. She is last.

My stomach rumbles. But I'm thirstier than anything else. I glance around, and Raj offers up a container that seems to be made of something like heavy canvas. The water goes down cold and sharp.

I wipe my mouth, and Raj grins at me. "Hungry?"

Giving him back the water, I wave a hand. "I… I don't think I've had a lot to eat lately."

His grin drops and his eyes narrow. "Skye said you don't really remember anything."

"I remember my name. I get…flashes." For a moment, I bite my lower lip and then ask, "Skye said something about a wipe. Do you think that's what's wrong with me? A bad wipe?"

His eyebrows rise up high. I notice they peak in the center—like the wings I see on the birds painted on the walls. "A wipe's supposed to remove sensitive data. Access codes, tech specs, that sort of thing. It's not supposed to take…well, everything. The AI is just careful."

Sitting up, I ask, "That's the second time someone's mentioned the AI. What is that? What's wrong with me? Why I was cast aside? Thrown away?"

Raj leans forward and rubs his lower lip. He glances at the other Glitches, but they are still talking to each other and ignoring us. His eyes seem very bright. I decide he is considering things. I like that.

He gives a nod and rubs his palms together. "The AI runs the Norm. I don't know much more than that. I don't think anyone does. But…you not remembering? You wouldn't be trashed for that."

"Why not?"

"Because the AI would be able to retrieve your memories or give you viable new ones that would allow you to interact with the other Techs. If there's one thing I know, the AI is all about preservation." The word comes out with an edge to it as if he is saying it but doesn't think it is true. "I don't think your memory was damaged. I think you were wiped for a reason. The real question is what makes you a Glitch in the first place?"

He pauses, eyebrows raised high and dark eyes intense. I can see he wants me to give him an answer, but I have none.

Sitting back, he smiles. "Unless, of course, you suffered permanent brain damage during the wipe."

My chest goes hollow. I can't seem to catch a breath. My fingers are numb and cold. Now I know there may be something really wrong with me—and there might not be anything I can do about it. Wolf might be right. The AI, and even Mother might be right.

It's all my fault and maybe I should be thrown away.

Chapter Five

I manage to eat a few bites. Skye keeps telling me I have to eat, but all my hunger has vanished. I don't even know if I'm worth the food I've been given.

Wolf comes over to us and tells me, "Croc has to check you for other things."

Standing, Raj's mouth pulls down. I can sense Raj plans to say something, but I stand between Raj and Wolf. "Let's go."

Without another word, Wolf turns and strides away. I follow. I have nothing better to do. The tunnels are dark, but I can find my way by keeping one hand on the stone. It's cool and smooth under my fingers.

Croc seems surprised to see me again, but Wolf gives a nod at me and says, "Bugs."

Lights now glow in some of the glass jars, making the room seem bright. I have no idea what Wolf's words mean. Maybe if I wait I'll find out.

With a shrug, Croc starts to poke at me, running his hands over my head, behind my ears and over my skin. Croc mutters about malnutrition, vitamin deficiencies, muscle atrophy but the words mean nothing to me. I stick out my tongue for him. He looks into my ears and shines a very bright light into my eyes.

He says the burns on my skin are healing much faster than he expected. Otherwise, I'm clean. He gives me something he calls ointment to put on my skin for the sunburn and tells me to drink lots of water, which earns him a scathing look from Wolf.

"There isn't a lot of water to go around." Wolf glances at me and back to Croc. "Alternatives?"

Croc sighs, like this is something that happens too much. "Cacti. Snake as raw as she'll take it. The cacti hold water well and the blood in the snake will help. It's the best I can do."

Making my voice hard, I tell Wolf, "I am right here."

Wolf nods at Croc and turns to me. Finally. "Go back to Skye. She'll show you where to sleep."

"Sleep?"

"Be nonfunctional—that's what you Glitches like to call it. Soon as your feet heal you're out to scavenge. We'll see if you're useful like Bird says."

"What exactly does that mean?"

Wolf shakes his head and turns away. "You'll learn. Or not."

When Wolf is gone, Croc pats my shoulder and offers a sympathetic smile. "Don't worry. He's a marshmallow inside."

"What's that?"

Croc stares at me and laughs. "Good one. Okay, so he's not really all that soft. But he's a good man. Trust him and he'll trust you. He's learned the hard way that this life is survival at any cost. The only thing that matters is that the clan goes on as a whole. Wolf lives by that."

I frown at this, not in the least convinced. "Thanks, but…something else has to matter." Leaving Croc, I find Skye is waiting for me.

"C'mon. Let's get some sleep." Skye slaps my arm. In the big room where we ate, there is no light shining down from the hole in the ceiling. I look up and see dark blue, and what looks like a white circle in the sky.

"Moon's full," Skye says. "Means we start a new cycle." I glance at her and she smiles and points to the light that is warm and bright within the circle of black stones. "That's a fire." She points up. "That's the full moon. This is the Center. Rogues track time by the moon—by how it shows up in the Center here over the fire. Least the Trackers do. Moon tells us when we need to scavenge when the dry season's coming—"

"It's not dry now?" The question bursts out of me. I'm exhausted, but I haven't done anything except get poked at by Croc.

Skye smiles. "It gets dryer. For now, we sleep—time to be nonfunctional for a few hours. The Trackers say it's a good sign if you dream of water. Means you'll get some." Turning, Skye leads me down another tunnel and to another cavern. It isn't as large, and the drawings are of plants of all kinds. Light filters into the room, thin and silver, from three holes in the ceiling. Air comes in, too, dry smelling and cool now. The floor is covered with squares of woven grass and cloth. A few cloths seem to have hair on them.

"Grab a fur," Skye says. "If you don't get one soon, they'll be gone. The furs are warmer than the blankets and it'll be cold by dawn." I don't know what she means, but she grabs a hairy cloth and pushes it at me and takes one for herself. Other females come into the room. The Rogues avoid us, but Bird does smile at me. Most seem very young.

"This is where the girls sleep unless you're in a mood to mate, and then you have to find a spot somewhere with your guy. But Rogues don't much care to be with a Glitch." Skye makes a face and then picks her way to a place against the far wall. "I sleep in the back near Chandra." She nods at the tall, lanky girl who ate with us earlier—the other Glitch. "We're not really close," Skye adds in a low whisper.

Chandra shoots us a look, her chin up and her face set in a blank look. She turns away, making it clear she isn't interested in Skye or me.

Spreading her fur, Skye puts her back to Chandra. She plops down on the fur, stretches, lies back and pulls the fur over her. "Dream of water, Lib," she mumbles.

Feeling out of place, I glance around again. Chandra has also gone nonfunctional…to sleep, as Wolf called it. Or at the least, lies with her back to me. I don't know why she seems so unfriendly. Doesn't she think we're the same?

Glancing around, I see the room is filled. I spot Bird. She lies on her back, her eyes open. She stares at the ceiling as if she sees more than stone. There's something about her that puts a shiver on my skin. But at least she was kind to me. Right now, that goes a long way.

As if sensing my stare, Bird turns and looks at me. She tips her head to the side. I feel like people have been doing that a lot lately.

With a hushed voice, she says, "Don't worry. You'll figure it out." She gives me that wide smile that engulfs her entire face.

Frowning, I ask, "What do you mean?"

Chandra hisses at me. Others shoot Bird a dirty look and roll away.

I decide it's useless to try and talk to anyone now. It's pretty clear everyone wants to sleep, so I let out a frustrated sigh and spread my fur.

Lying down, my brain keeps working. I want to pull out memories, but how can I? There's so much I still don't know. My eyes seem to have weights on them. They close and then…

I'm yelling at them to run, but they are screaming and yelling. There's nowhere to go. Mud, thick and clogging spills in the holes above us.

"Lib!"

I recognize the voice. It's Wolf. My heart thuds in my chest. I turn in a circle, searching for him. All I see are dark forms, struggling to get away from the mud that maybe isn't mud. It's too black. And it's hot and sticky.

"Lib?" Wolf shouts.

I try to answer, but the pouring black heat is filling the room, clogging the tunnel.

Everyone is dying.

I swallow and foul bile burns my throat. Skye's golden hair is coated in oily black. Raj tries to scramble up the wall but falls back into the blackness and I know there is no saving him.

"Lib, here!"

I swivel toward the voice and see Wolf reaching for me. His muscular arm is extended toward me. Black patches cover his skin, but he's fought his way to me.

"Wolf!" I call for him. Mouth set into a hard line, he stares at me and then at the blackness around him. Too late, I realize he is trying to save me.

I'm the only one here who doesn't need saving.

"No!" I yell. But he's already jumped into the muck. He screams as the heat burns through his clothing to reach bare skin. It doesn't stop him. He struggles toward me. And now I wonder if it is so he can wrap his hands around my throat to end my existence.

The blackness covers him, spreading up his body until all that's visible is his face. I'm shaking. My chest hurts. Wetness streaks down my face.

Everything seems to slow. The world grows quiet. A voice spreads through the silence. It is not Wolf's, not mine, and not the screams of the dying.

"You must do the right thing, Lib." Her words are soothing.

Even though terror surrounds me, though everything is wrong, though there is nothing left of Wolf or Skye or Raj, I smile and…

I take a breath as though I have been holding stale air in my lungs for too long. It hurts. I cough and sit up. My coughs echo off the walls. Looking around, I realize I am surrounded by sleeping Rogues. I'm also sweating and shaking.

Shivering now, I glance around to see who I've woken. I don't see anyone stirring. I let out a breath.

But then Bird sits up. She glances over at me, her dark eyes huge and glinting in the dim light. "Don't worry." Her voice sounds as if she is far away. Maybe she is still dreaming, too. "The storm won't hit us. Not this time. No one will drown."

I frown at her. A flash of light whitens the room. It's enough to startle me and I let out a gasp. I clamp a hand over my mouth. Rumbling follows the light.

"Lightning. But no rain with it this time," Bird says.

"How do you know?" I ask.

Bird smiles, lies down and is sleeping again just like that.

Glancing once more at the holes to the outside world, I wonder about the storm, about Bird, and about the flood of blackness slipping into the room. And I envy Bird.

I also don't allow myself to be nonfunctional again while it is dark.

Chapter Six

Several days pass and I keep myself busy enough that the dreams do no more than leave me weary in the morning. Life begins to seem more familiar. I never stray far from the other Glitches, but Chandra and Marq have little to say to me. The only Rogues who talk to me are Bird and Croc—and sometimes Wolf. He doesn't seem to like me, or maybe that's the wrong way to put it. Maybe it's about anger…or trust. He doesn't seem to have much to say to the other Glitches, either. Skye and Raj tell me to stay out of Wolf's path, but the caverns are small and there is only so much avoiding I can do.

Sometimes during meals, Bird tells everyone stories of the clans. She has lots of stories about how the clans got their names, but to me, they all sound like tales. It makes me even more aware that I have no stories. I think about making some up. But now I've found other Glitches, what am I supposed to do? It seems to me I should know. Maybe that means I haven't found all the others, or enough. But I am stuck in the caverns for now, so I focus on rubbing the cream Croc gave me into my feet several times a day, going to see Croc to talk to him, and spending time with Skye.

Skye finds me cloth to put on my feet—boots she calls them. She traded some gear she didn't want for them. I don't know what gear is, but the boots are soft and make walking easier on my feet. Skye also gives me cloth for my legs—pants. She says most of the Rogues wear skins, not cloth. That sounds horrible to me, but I have to admit the fur skins make sleeping warmer.

Croc approves of my new clothes and says I'm healed enough to scavenge now. He seems surprised about both things. "I've never seen anyone recover this fast." He rubs a thumb over his cheek as if he doesn't know what else to say. I don't know either. He's frowning as I leave his cavern, but I think he is more curious than troubled.

At least I hope so.

In the Center, five Rogues sit near the stones that usually hold fire. Light pours in through the hole in the ceiling, so no other light is needed during the day. The Rogues don't look my way, but I spot Skye and Raj and head over to where they stand against the far wall.

When I reach Skye, she asks, "What'd Croc say?"

Raj leans against the cavern wall, careful not to touch any of the drawings. No one touches the drawings, but Bird sometimes waves at them when she is telling stories. Tipping his head to one side, Raj waits for my answer.

I tug at the cloth that covers my chest. It's my old one and I wish it fit better. "Croc said I'm fine." I don't mention what he said about my fast healing. My mind isn't healing so fast, so maybe my body is making up for that. Besides, all Glitches are supposed to have something wrong with them. Wolf said Skye was unstable—but I haven't seen that. Chandra and Marq don't talk much, so maybe that's what's wrong with them. I have a bad memory, but Raj doesn't seem to have anything wrong with him.

Raj pushes off the wall and nods once. "Wolf wants to go out today."

I glance up at the light pouring down the hole and ask, "Will it be hot?"

Raj nods again. "Yeah. But we can keep to the shadows as much as possible. And you don't want to miss this. It's the way Rogues survive out here."

"And we prove we're useful," Skye says.

"Enough that Wolf lets us stay." Raj's voice deepens with a bitterness I have not seen in him before. Remembering Raj's argument with Wolf my first night here, I decide they don't get along.

"What are we supposed to scavenge? And where? I mean—I saw the ruins when Skye and I walked here, but it didn't seem like much was there."

Skye pulls off the cloth that covers her arms—her jacket, she calls it. "Use this. You'll find something good. Glitches just know where to find gear. I don't get to go this time." Her mouth pulls down and her eyebrows flatten.

Raj glances at her and says, "If you hadn't split off from everyone last time and brought back a stranger after sundown, you wouldn't be left behind this time."

Eyes narrowing, she folds her arms across her chest and sticks out her tongue at him. Then she smiles. My chest tightens and I rub it with my fingers. I want to be like Skye—to know I can smile and make fun of others. But I feel as if I am still not really sure of my place. All I have is a purpose—and I don't know what to do with it.

Turning his back on Skye, Raj tells me, "You're coming. Skye's not. But I'll be with you to show you the program."

He winks at me and heads off to one of the tunnels. I still haven't figured out where they all lead.

I start to follow, but Skye grabs the sleeve of her jacket, which I now hold. "Don't worry. Raj knows what he's doing. He'll watch out for you. And don't let Wolf see you sweat."

She jerks a thumb to one side. I glance over and see Wolf watching me. He wears his skins, just like always. But today his arms are bare and I see more muscles. It's as if he wants to look intimidating. And he does. His size seems to swallow up the room, though that's ridiculous, but there's just something about him that is larger than everything else.

When my gaze meets his, Wolf seems to hold very still for a moment. But he turns away and starts down the tunnel Raj took.

Skye gives my back a push. "Later."

I follow Wolf, rushing to catch up with him, glad I have boots. The floors are always cold in the caverns.

Somehow Wolf knows when I'm right behind him. Without looking back, he shoves a bag at me. It has one long strap and a flap covers a large pocket.

I take it and ask, "What's this for?" Wolf wears one just like this, slung across his body. I put on the pouch the same way.

Wolf doesn't even glance at me. "It's for whatever you find out there. Don't lose it."

"What if I find something that won't fit?"

He stops so fast I almost run into his back. Turning, he stares at me, his dark eyes glittering in the light from behind us in the Center. My face warms. But I will not look away from him. It seems like I see something that might be humor in his eyes. It disappears too fast for me to be certain.

He pushes a finger against my breast bone. "Stay close. Do what you're told. Don't make me regret this."

"The way I am now?" I mutter.

Turning, Wolf strides down the tunnel again. I have to jog to keep up with him, but when I'm close I ask, "What if I don't want to go? I mean, I do, but does anyone ever say no?" Glancing at Wolf's back, I see his shoulders hunch slightly. Just how much can I push him? I am tired of staying out of his way and being the one who shouldn't be noticed.

Wolf glances back at me. His eyes seem darker and they narrow. His nostrils flare, but his voice comes out slow and soft. "It's out with us or you're welcome to go out on your own. Everyone gets to make a choice." He strides away.

My steps falter, but only few. I think about what Bird said about the group being important. That still doesn't seem right to me. What about each person? There's no time to even think about arguing, so I hurry after Wolf. The tunnel turns and twists, but I can hear the slap of Wolf's boots on the hard stone. It grows dark this deep in the tunnel and I have to feel for the wall to find my way. Maybe we're heading for the hole I came through my first night here.

The tunnel turns and light blooms as the walls fall back into a space that is not quite a room. I have to blink to adjust my sight, but Raj and Bird, Bear, and two other Rogues—a female and a male—stand in the center under a hole where light shines down.

Bird grins at me and Wolf waves a curt gesture at the other Rogues. "Bobcat and Lion, and you'll remember Bear."

I give Wolf a long stare. Is he making a joke about me remembering Bear? He isn't smiling, but his eyes are bright again. I am sure he's laughing inside—at me. I glance at the Rogues. Bobcat is the female. She is almost as tall as Bear, though nowhere near as wide. Lion—the male—just stares at me, his expression empty. He dresses like Wolf in skins and his tawny hair is almost as wild as Bird's, but he doesn't have ribbons in it.

Wolf turns to the Rogues and says, "Lib's new. She'll stay with Raj. Keep an eye on her."

The girl, Bobcat, fixes a stare on me and her dislike washes over me like a cold wind. She is tall and skinny with short dark hair and dark eyes in a narrow face. Everything about her seems pulled thin. Bear ignores me, and Lion turns away to go with Wolf. So does Bird.

I glance at the floor, my cheeks burning now even though I have not been in the sun. They don't want me here. They don't like me. But I have nowhere else to go, and I am determined now to prove I can be useful. Then they'll want me here.

Wolf strides down yet another tunnel and the Rogues follow. Feet dragging, I start walking, too. Raj falls into step next to me.

"Where are we going?" I ask in a whisper because no one else is talking.

Raj shakes his head and puts a finger to his lips. It seems we're not supposed to talk.

The tunnel goes on a long way. It's dusty walking behind the others. I have to swallow to keep from coughing. It's dry and there's nothing here to scavenge. The tunnel darkens. Raj bumps his elbow into me every now and then to help me not walk into a wall.

At last I see light ahead again. The tunnel widens once more. I have to squint. I am used to seeing only the darkness. The tunnel stops suddenly. Looking around, I just see walls and a hole overhead. Nothing else.

Wolf steps into the circle of sunlight that leaks down from the hole. He reaches above him and pulls. A rope falls into the dust. Knots are tied at regular intervals and make the rope seem heavy.

Leaning over to Raj, I whisper, "I don't know if I can climb."

Bear shoots me an annoyed look, but Raj puts his hand on my shoulder and squeezes. Skye said Raj would look after me, so I have to trust that.

Wolf goes up first. He jumps up, grabs the rope and goes hand over hand, quick and efficient. He makes it seem easy and I can't help but admire his skill as he disappears through the hole. I expect another Rogue to go up after Wolf, but they stand still, bodies tensed, staring up at the light.

I turn to ask Raj why we're waiting, but a rock drops down into the hole. It hits the dirt with a puff of dust. A second rock falls. Bear reaches down and sweeps up both rocks. He chucks them back up through the hole.

This time, only one falls back down again. It has to be a message of some kind, and I start to wonder what's outside that makes the Rogues so cautious.

With a glance upward, Bear grabs the rope and climbs out. Bobcat goes next, moving even faster than Bear or Wolf. Lion grabs the rope, tugs on it once and goes up, and Bird follows him up. She grins at me before using both her hands and her feet to climb the rope.

Raj motions for me to go up next. He'll go last. I nod, glad that I'm not going to be the last one out and left here to struggle out on my own.

Grabbing the rope, I find it's rougher than it looks. Harsh against my palms. Am I strong enough to climb? My stomach ties a larger knot than those on the rope. I gulp down a breath and look up. Closing my eyes, I see again what the others did—jump, pull, wrap my ankles around the rope, get a boot on a knot, grab and pull and push. Opening my eyes, I find I'm already at the top.

Sunlight beats down on me, warming my scalp. I swing there for a moment, and a strong hand reaches down, grabs Skye's jacket by the shoulder, and hauls me up and out.

Wolf keeps hold of me. I'm on my feet now, but so close to him I can smell his scent. It's musky and I want to lean closer to breathe it in so I'll always know this. I stare at him, blinking in the sudden brightness of the sun. Wolf seems almost a dark shadow, but the sunlight brings golden touches to his skin and hair. He looks away and drops his hands from me. I sway and almost want to grab for him, but that would make me seem weak.

Instead, I straighten and turn to watch Raj come up out of the hole. Lion grabs Raj and pulls him out. At least I'm not the only Glitch being hauled around.

Wolf squints as he looks around. He gives a nod and starts to walk in a direction. We follow.

Everything is what I remember from my walk here with Skye—dusty ground, hard rock, distant mountains that seem almost purple. Every now and then metal juts up from the land, twisted and bent and shimmering in the sun. For a moment, other images flash in front of me—green and smooth paths and people walking past, hurrying with purpose, their cloth tunics fluttering. Is it a memory?

My mouth is already dry.

We keep walking until we reach a space that is straight and smooth. A road. The word pops into my head. On either side of it, rock walls rise up, striped by sediment and years of erosion. Cool shadows wash over the road. Stepping out of the sun, I let out a breath and glance back.

The hole we climbed out of has disappeared. Now I see why Bird said we need each other. I would never find my way back on my own. Ahead of Raj and me, the Rogues keep walking, glancing up at the sky every now and then.

Glancing at Raj, I ask, "What are they looking for?"

He looks at the sky and then says, his voice soft and low, "We make a point of not making noise when we're going in and out. And we're all watching or listening for drones."

An image hovers close—something black in the air, something like the sentinel I saw within the platform after the connect, but round. "Drones." I let the word roll around my tongue, hoping it will stir more memories, but nothing comes to me.

Raj gives a low laugh. "You really don't know anything."

Pushing my shoulders back, I shoot him a sideways glance. "Hey, I know things."

He actually laughs, and Bird glances back, her eyes bright as if she wants to be in on whatever is funny. Leaning closer, Raj whispers, "Right, you know your name."

Raj doesn't smell as good as Wolf, but his scent is nice, too. It stirs something in my memory, but it slips away too fast. Does he smell like electronics? Brushed metal? My cheeks warm, and I put a hand up to shade my face. "I know your name, too."

He nudges my shoulder with his. Bobcat calls back, her voice a low hiss, "Keep up!"

It seems we walk a long way, following this road that isn't quite a road, past rocks and sand and sand and rocks. The ground starts to rise. Sweat beads on my forehead and slicks my back. I haven't breath to talk, so I focus on one foot in front of the other. Raj's boots and mine make a shuffling sound, but the Rogues walk in utter silence. At last we come to a rise, and Wolf lifts a hand. Everyone stops. Bird pulls out a bulging skin. The Rogues pass it around. When it comes to Raj, I can smell the water. Raj drinks only a little and passes the skin to me. I want to drink it all, but I copy Raj and only drink a little. I pass the skin back to Bird and turn away.

In the distance, the wall rises up. I can't see the platform where I met Skye, but I know it must be there, dwarfed by that metallic, gray wall, which spans the horizon.

I turn to Raj and ask, "Are we heading there? For water?" I lick my lips. That was what Skye had said she'd wanted to get—water. It seems to be the rarest thing in the world.

Will going back to the wall or one of the platforms help my memory?

Raj shifts the strap to his pouch and adjusts it. His dark skin gleams and his scent seems stronger now. He wipes the beads of moisture from his face. "Mostly water. We probably won't find any the AI doesn't control, but we're looking for food, too. Snake, lizard and yucca or cacti if we can find them. Gear, too. Pieces left out to rust or anything that might be useful. You just never know. If we're lucky we might find a big cat or a few rabbits. But the main thing is water."

An image flashes into mind—blue pooling water. My body aches with longing. It's such a lovely picture. I don't want to banish the image, but it's distracting.

Raj's words—harsh and hard—pull me back to the hot sun and the barren land. "The AI's gone wrong. It's the real glitched system."

Confused now, I glance at him.

He lifts a hand. "Sort of. Mostly, the AI needs water—we all do. The Norm can't survive without it. So the AI hoards it, just like it does with everything." He gestures with a hand to the rocks and sand and twisted ruins. "It looks like this because of the AI. There used to be huge cities and plants, trees, grass—but the AI takes everything. One of these days, we'll get to the AI's core and bring it back in line. We'll make it work right again."

The skin on the back of my neck prickles. Biting my lower lip, I'm not sure why Raj's words leave me so uneasy. I shift on my feet and glance at the huge wall. That must be the Norm. I know that. But the AI—I'm not really sure who or what that is. And why would the AI want to take everything from the world?

Licking my lips, I glance around again. The dry heat seems to want to suck the water from me. The sand shifts under my boots.

Why does the AI want everything this world has to give?

A shiver slips down my back again. Turning away from the wall—the Norm—I don't want to talk about it or even think about it right now. It just seems overwhelming. Like Raj, I shift the pouch strap and say, "My feet are already beginning to ache."

At this, Raj smiles. "Mine, too. But, well, you'll see. It's not much farther. We just don't want to leave what we have too close to any Central." He looks at the sky. "It's not safe."

My skin prickles again. There is danger out here, danger that I don't really know about. I look at the sky, too, but I see only pale blue. The wind picks up, pushing my hair into my eyes, brushing heat and stinging sand over my skin. It whistles through the rocks behind us.

Wolf gives a wave and we start walking again.

The road turns down and into a very narrow space that at last opens out just like the tunnels did. Straggly plants grow here. The ground is flat, too, and I realize this is part of a platform, but the metal is hidden under sand.

Two boulders squat next to the sandy platform. There's something odd about them. I tip my head to one side and squint. They don't seem natural. Wolf reaches for one boulder and grabs it. He gives one jerk. I gasp. The illusion is shattered. The rock becomes dirt-colored cloth and reveals a small box with black, metal bars around four large tires and a seat that might be leather or canvas. Edging closer, careful not to touch it, I glance at a single set of handlebars that jut up. What might be a light sits on the front. It's a vehicle. I glance at Wolf, irritation stirring like an itch under my skin. He couldn't have told me?

"See? No more walking," Raj tells me and nudges my side with his elbow.

I glance at him. "You couldn't have told me?" I let my irritation out at him. Raj's smile fades. I glance back at the vehicles.

There are three of them…and seven of us, and it doesn't look like these cages on wheels are designed to hold three people. That would leave one person still on foot.

"Bird rides with me," Wolf announces. He reaches into his pouch and pulls out something that looks like a bunch of wires. He untangles them and hands them out. I glance around. Others are putting them on their heads. "Speak through headsets, but keep it short. Batteries don't last forever. Raj, you keep the new Glitch."

"Lib." Raj says the word with a sharp bite in his tone.

Wolf just keeps talking. "Bobcat and Bear, ride together. Lion, you're scout. If there's trouble, run. Use the supplies judiciously."

Lion nods, but I am still staring at the headset and trying to make sense of everything. Lion scrambles up and over some of the actual boulders and disappears from sight. That's why we only need three cages on wheels.

I turn to Raj. "Where did he—?"

"Lion's scout, so he'll stay here. If we don't make it back before dark, he'll run and tell the rest of the clan and they'll move."

I want to ask him more. Where will they move? What about all the tunnels, will they have to make more? And why wouldn't we come back? But Wolf has already climbed onto one of the vehicles and Bird slips behind him, wrapping her arms around his waist to hold on. Bobcat and Bear are similarly paired, and Bobcat is in front with what looks like the controls.

Raj helps me put on my headset and motions for me to follow him. The headset has one part that sits over my right ear and something else close enough to my mouth to touch skin. I figure it's something I can talk into and hear others through.

Climbing onto the vehicle, Raj does something and it wakes with a hum. I slide on. The vehicle vibrates underneath me.

"Hold on," Raj says. I slide my arms around his middle, holding him only loosely. Wolf takes off in a cloud of dust.

Raj makes the vehicle leap forward with a roar. I tighten my grip around Raj. He's lean and hard to hold. Wind whips into my face. I can see why we have headsets now. The wind makes it impossible to talk without them.

I'm not sure the vehicles are better than walking. My feet feel better, but they kick up sand that stings my face. I'm glad I have pants and boots and Skye's jacket to cover my arms. I duck my head behind Raj and that helps but I can't see much.

We bounce over the ground, my butt hitting the seat and my teeth shaking from the ride. Raj seems determined to stay right on Wolf's tail and Bobcat skims over the ground next to us.

Wolf's voice crackles over the headset. "Bird, are you getting anything?"

After a pause, Bird says, "Head east to the Tower."

Leaning forward, I ask Raj, "What's the Tower?"

He waves a hand—he hasn't heard—and tells me, "Use the buttons. Green will let you talk to me. Red lets you talk to everyone."

I fiddle with the buttons. They're small and I don't want to let go of Raj. If I do, I'll probably fall. That doesn't sound fun to me. Finding the right button, I ask the question again and tell him, "I remember… some things. Flashes of things. But not the tower."

Over the headset, he asks, "Why do you think they're malfunctioning like that?"

"Malfunctioning?"

"Your memories."

"That's a weird question." My throat tightens and I think of how Bird had said human before. Leaning against Raj's back, I ask, "Why do you say malfunctioning? Like they're something that's broken? Is that a Glitch thing?"

"Sort of," he answers. His voice sounds odd over the headset—distant and higher than normal. But he doesn't seem bothered by this. "Every Tech is part machine. We have gear added on to give us abilities to connect. A Glitch is a Tech that's failing in some way. That's why the Rogues don't like us around. Some clans won't even take in a Glitch. We're part gene-spliced and part gear. That lets us hack the AI systems, but that's not always good. The AI's always watching for unauthorized connects."

My skin is prickling. Half human…I'm part gear. That leaves me thinking about how my skin seems smoother than that of any

Rogue. Too smooth maybe. And is my fast healing because I'm different?

I think about how Skye was having trouble with her connect when I found her, and I ask, "So Rogues keep us around because we can hack better than they can?"

"Makes us useful," he says.

Cold settles in my stomach. I'm useful if I can hack, but what if I'm too broken for that? I bury my face against Raj's back again, letting the cloth rub my cheek. I can hack. I helped Skye out of trouble. So I am useful. And I also don't feel like I'm part gear. I eat and sleep and need water and have feelings. So what makes me different? My malfunctioning memory?

Wolf's voice comes over the headset in a low growl. "Platform ahead. Raj, time to do your thing."

My stomach stays in knots. I tighten my hold on Raj. He is useful. We all are. But why can't he be of value just because he exists?

Raj slows the vehicle and stops it next to Wolf and Bird's vehicle.

I slide off, my legs and chest still vibrating from the rough ride. Sand clings to my eyelashes and I spit out more sand. My eyes sting from the dust and wind, though Raj thankfully blocked most of it.

I blink and take a look at the platform.

We're close to the wall, and there is a tower here that juts up into the sky — round and smooth and seems to have no function. The platform looks like the one Skye tried to hack. But the silver-gray metal looks rusted in spots. The platform is also leaning to one side as if it's sinking into the ground. Shards of glass surround it and a few more shards cling to metal frames. Inside the glass and metal, the same railing stands out. That's our connect. I'm hoping Raj is better at this than Skye was.

Wolf glances around. Bobcat and Bear pull up and their vehicle shuts off, too, as soon as it stops. I don't know what powers these vehicles, but whatever it is leaves them quiet with only a soft hum when they run.

Seeming satisfied with what he's seen—or hasn't seen—Wolf waves Raj forward. "See if you can't get water from it." All the Rogues, except Bird, seem tense. They keep glancing around, and Bobcat and Bear have spread out. Wolf keeps glancing at the tower as if he expects something to burst out of it, but it—like the platform—looks battered to me. Scarred with red and black streaks as if it's been in a fight with something.

Looking at the platform again, I'm not sure the connect will work here.

Raj swings off his vehicle and steps through one of the broken panels that doesn't have any glass shards sticking out. He braces his legs wide to stand against the tilting floor.

Interested now, I stretch up on tiptoes to see what he does. He'll take hold of the railing, just as Skye and I did. But will he do anything else.

The back of my neck tingles and I get an itch between my shoulder blades. Turning, I see Wolf watching me. His eyes aren't gleaming now but look flat, dark, and unreadable. But I know what he's thinking.

He's wondering if I'm too broken to be useful like the Glitches. He's thinking Skye made up a story about me saving her so he'd have to take me in.

Lifting my chin, I stare back at him and say, my voice flat, "I know how to hack. I just want to see if Raj has a different style."

He huffs out a breath, turns and walks away to stand with his back to the platform as if he's looking for trouble to come our way. Maybe the Rogues are watching for drones. I'm not sure. I do know Raj may hit a sentinel inside the hack—just like Skye did.

Turning back, I wet my lips and watch Raj. He brushes off the railing, clearing away the dust. He rubs his palms together and glances up at the tower once before putting both hands on the railing.

And nothing happens.

Raj stands still, his head tipped back and his eyes closed. But under his eyelids, I can see his eyes moving. He's looking. He's someplace else, the way Skye was in that cool, blue room.

The wind shifts and starts to blow harder. It pushes sand into my face and eyes, and I have to turn and put my back to it. My hair slaps my face and the world smells dry and hot. The wind's hot, too.

Wolf shifts and moves back to sit on the cage on wheels. Tension stiffens his shoulders. To either side, Bobcat and Bear watch the sky. Bird walks over, her boots silent on the sand, and stands next to me.

"It always seems to take a long time. Waiting, that is," Bird says.

I lift a shoulder. "I don't mind waiting." I look from her to Wolf. Bird seems to know him better than anyone, so I ask, "Is that why Wolf doesn't like Glitches? We take too long to do things and he'd rather be the one hacking? Not that I care what he thinks."

Bird glances at me, her eyes sharp. The wind flutters the ribbons in her hair, snapping them. "You don't care? Really?"

Folding my arms over my chest, I keep my stare on Raj. His face is beaded with moisture now. "Why should I? I'm only half human."

She makes a sound that could be a short laugh or could be a snort. And she leans closer. "Sometimes Wolf's just difficult. Aren't we all?"

I'm not really satisfied by this answer. I look at her and try to read her face to see if she's making a joke, but her expression suddenly goes blank and her eyes become distant. It's as though she is looking somewhere far away and thinking of something else.

"Bird?" I put a hand on her narrow shoulder and shake her a little. "Bird?"

Wolf's voice makes me jump. "What's going on?"

Glancing over, I see he's come right up to us and stands on my other side. I didn't hear him move. I shake my head. "She just…it's like she's in the connect, too. Or someplace else."

Turning to Bird, Wolf lowers his voice and softens his tone more than I thought he could. "What do you see?"

She answers in a soft, sing-song voice. "Storm coming. Fast. Can't stay." She turns her face into the wind.

I turn, too, and see brown clouds darkening the sky. Beyond them, it looks black. In the distance, a white line lashes down from the clouds. Lightning. The word pops into my head along with the danger. It's wild electricity—erratic and dangerous. This lightning could be what's wrecked the platform and the tower, too.

Wolf stares at the clouds as if he sees more than I do—maybe even more than Bird. With a look at where Raj is still hacking the system, Wolf says, "We need to get moving."

"You can't leave Raj behind," I tell him.

Bird blinks once, twice, and seems to be aware of me now. She turns to Wolf and says, "Send her in after him."

Wolf gives her a sharp look. So do I and lift my eyebrows high. My mouth dries and my fingertips tingle. I want this, and yet I'm worried. I'm not sure I want to deal with another sentinel.

"Send her in." Bird makes the words firmer this time.

Wolf is looking at me, not Bird. Bear and Bobcat are still out, staring at the sky and now at the clouds heading our way.

I give a nod. "I saved Skye. I can help Raj."

Wolf frowns as if he's not sure he thinks I can do this—or not sure he wants me to try.

Before he can question my skills, I walk to the platform, slip in through the broken panel Raj used, and place one hand next to Raj's with our littlest fingers touching.

In a blink, I'm in.

Chapter Seven

The world inside the connect seems just like the outside, but more complex. Making a Connection—hacking—is like walking through a doorway for me. I don't know if that is how it is for all Glitches, but that's how it is for me.

I grip the railing, turn it, and just push.

Connection: Secure.

I walk into a room so wide and long I can't see the walls. Aisles of cabinets stretch out before me in a filing system of some kind. Here I know things without having to know. It's as if my memories are here and flood back into me. In here, everything is calmer, cooler. The connect is comforting in a way that is unlike anything else.

The room is blue again and gives light enough to see. No sun is needed. The entire room glows on its own with a soft, blue glimmer that is easy on my eyes, which really means it is my mind seeing all this.

For a moment, I just want to stand and absorb. This is familiar to me. I almost forget why I'm here. But something nudges me.

Find Raj.

It's odd because it's as if Wolf spoke those words to me. But he's not here. Raj isn't either.

Where is he? He's taking too long and a storm is coming. That flash of lightning I saw leaves me jittery inside. I do not want to be inside a connect with wild electricity bursting around me. If it fried the tower, it could do worse to me inside a connect. I know that with a knowing that lives in my bones.

Scanning the room, I look for signs of where Raj might be. Last connect, Skye stood right in front of me. Good news is that while Raj isn't here, no sentinels are here, either.

I start searching.

If Raj is looking for water, I should, too.

Time is different here—I know this. So is movement. I think of a place and am just there. I wonder if I could think of Raj and find him that way.

I look at the filing cabinets. I need to speed this up. Not only is time different here, I am different.

I close my eyes. When I open them, the world has changed slightly. Threads of thin light now connect the files and cabinets. Lifting a hand, light stretches from me to everything inside this world. I reach out and pluck one of the strings with a careful finger. It vibrates, sending ripples that quickly fade. One thread hits something that isn't a wall, but also is. A firewall. Behind the wall, I'll find a panel. I know this, just as I know I can touch the threads of this world.

The firewall doesn't hold me out. I slip through it, following more threads. It's as if I can fold myself sideways to fit between the wall that is there and isn't. Quantum, I think. More than one state—just like me.

At the panel, I place my hand on it. More threads flow into my fingertips and code appears, riding the lines of light. The list isn't in a code language anyone speaks, but it is in one I understand. Memories surface, but I'm looking for water and Raj. The two are linked.

The code shifts into a fast blur. It's searching on my inquiry.

The list stops. Yellow glows around a single item, blinking on and off like a heartbeat. That's what I want. Something rumbles. I glance around to see the cabinets are rotating. They turn and twist and now I see Raj in the midst of the files.

Raj clings to one cabinet. I call his name without calling it.

He glances down at me when I call his name. "Lib? What's happening? Why are you here? You're going to alert the sentinels."

"No. The water's coming to us. Why didn't you just request it?"

His eyebrows flatten over his dark eyes and his mouth pulls down. I think he's going to say something, but he just turns away and climbs down the files.

The water pours down into a perfect cube. The edges glow and inside the water moves in ripples and waves. The cube rests in front of me. I place my hand on the surface. It glows brighter and the water disappears as though being siphoned off. I can't see where it's going, but I know I've directed it to come out of the Tower port into a container.

Raj drops down next to me. He stares at the cube and then looks at me. "How did you do that?"

I blink and shrug. "I don't understand your inquiry, but we have to disconnect. A storm is coming. It's got wild electricity."

He pales a little. "Let's go."

I give a nod. I close my eyes and open them.

Gone are the cool, blue room and the cube of slowly disappearing water. I'm back in dry heat and a biting wind, standing on a tilted platform. For an instant, longing almost chokes me. I want to go back—I want the connect.

I turn from the railing before I'm tempted to touch it again and go back. Glancing at Raj, I see his face is tight, and I think he feels the same as I do. We both want to be back inside. But we've been thrown out once. If we go back, we risk the sentinels coming after us.

Wolf for once is grinning. Seeing his teeth gleam and his eyes glitter pulls me fully back to the moment and out of the lingering desire to connect again.

“Don’t know how you did that, but it’s amazing!” Wolf slaps Raj’s shoulder, pauses, and then slaps mine.

I glance over to see Bear and Bobcat hauling containers from the tower and fastening them to the back of the vehicles.

We got the water Wolf wanted.

And now I’m not really sure how that happened. My memories of the blue room are fading already. I saw things…did things…but it seems I left my memories behind.

Glancing at the rail, I want to grab it again, but Bird grabs me instead and drags me from the platform. She spins me around. “I told you she was important.” Bird grins as if pleased with herself for doing something amazing.

Raj is staring at me. Bear and Bobcat are slapping his shoulder just like Wolf did, as if Raj did all of this. But Raj’s face is still tight and his eyes seem wary. I don’t like the look on his face, so I just turn away. The air snaps with the dry scent of ozone. I know the smell of electricity in the air.

“We need to go,” I tell Wolf.

Wolf waves to the others. Bear and Bobcat have the containers of water fastened to the vehicles.

"Let's ride the storm," Bird announces and claps her hands. She does another spin, her wild hair and ribbons whirling.

Wolf glances at her and then at the sky. "There's not enough time to get back."

Head tipped to one side, Bird smiles and shrugs. "Not enough time means enough time to reach the caves."

Wolf nods and waves to the others. "Send up a light air to let Lion know we're okay but can't make it."

Bobcat pulls out something flat and fastens it to a hose. It fills with something—a gas maybe—and turns into a silver sphere. Bobcat lets it go and the silver flies into the sky. The wind pushes it higher.

Glancing at the sky, I can see the clouds coming toward us, but it seems to me we have enough time to get back to the tunnels. Everyone is already on their cages on wheels, leaving me staring at the platform, at the dome wall, at the tower.

"Come on," Bird yells. "You don't want to miss the fun."

Chapter Eight

This is not fun.

The storm follows like a monster swallowing the sky. Explosions of light and thunderous noise shake the world and vibrate inside my chest. My hair seems to stand on end. Lightning strikes down and shoots back up from the ground. The storm drives rain with a furious wind. The whole thing moves so fast that fear seems a very wise reaction. Though Raj sends his vehicle over the ground at crazy speeds, a tightness wraps around my chest. I was wrong about having enough time. We're not going to make it.

Ahead, little black holes in a cliff face seem to be where we're heading. We race over the sand, but it seems a long way to the cliff, and the storm is overhead now. Dust swirls around, choking me and leaving me almost blind. How do the others know where to go? Ice and pebbles spit at us, stinging where they hit on my skin. It feels as if the world is turning inside out.

I press my face into Raj's back and have to work hard just to breathe.

Raj sends the cage vehicle faster. It's almost like he can sense I'm afraid…or maybe his own fear of the storm is pushing him to demand more. Raj's vehicle stays up next to Wolf's. At times I think the wheels will touch and lock, and we'll all end up eating dirt and spilling water. But Wolf always managed to veer away at the right time. I don't think this is a play for power between them or either of them showing off. Everyone's faces are set into grim determination. Even Bobcat keeps up with the others, leaning forward, her hair streaming back.

The water sloshes behind me. It's what we've risked everything for, but we might move faster without the extra weight. It seems a bad choice—die for water now or die because there is no water later.

The vehicle shoots up over a small dune and lands on two wheels. Raj leans to one side to bring the two spinning tires back onto the ground. Dust cakes my mouth and eyes. Glancing back, it looks as if there is nothing but brown behind us.

In the next instant, we're in one of the caves. Daylight has already faded into a brown twilight. Now the cave leaves the world even darker.

The storm tries to follow us inside, but the cave narrows and twists, and the storm runs out of energy before it can find us.

Slowing, Raj flicks on a switch and a light glows from the front of the vehicle. He brings the cage vehicle to a stop.

I'm shaking and clinging to him. The others stop their vehicles and they shut down. Except for everyone's ragged breathing, it's silent. My heart thunders in my chest and I just want to be back in that calm, blue room. I also don't want to let go of Raj.

"It's okay," Raj tells me, twisting around a little. His voice seems soft and reassuring. He pats my hand. The comforting gesture is enough to get me to relax a little. With my face warm, I release my death grip on him.

"Sorry," I mutter and swing off the vehicle.

Raj climbs off the vehicle, moving slowly as if his muscles hurt from having to keep that cage vehicle upright and moving fast. After a moment, my eyes adjust to the dimness. It will take longer to get used to the howling of the storm that rages behind us. No one seems to want to talk, and that's fine with me. Shoulders slumping, I sit on the hard rock floor.

This cave isn't like the expansive tunnels where the clan lives. From what I can see of the walls, they're rough, black stone. The floor is strewn with more rocks and a few bones. Maybe this is what a new tunnel looks like when the clan moves and has to make new tunnels.

My breathing slows and I ask, "Are we safe?" My voice echoes against the rocks.

Wolf stands by his cage vehicle, one hand on the water. "For now."

Bobcat and Bear gather rocks and set them into a ring. Bobcat pulls small bits of wood from the back of her cage vehicle and Bear gets a fire going. They don't talk as they work. They just get things done. The light is welcome. It casts odd shadows to the back of the cave, but it warms the space. And I like the bright, yellow flames. Once the fire is going, Bear shuts off all the vehicle lights.

"We'll spend the night," Wolf says. He settles down next to the fire.

"Why don't we head back after the storm passes? It'll be dark and cool. Don't you want to get the water back?"

Bobcat turns to stare at me. "Drones will be out. Looking for that water. They see fine at night and we don't, but the AI's going to be missing what we took. We'll go out when it's the hottest time. The AI never thinks we'll do that."

The fire is small, built with dry wood so there is little smoke. The Rogues sit close to it, but Raj sits next to me, his back against the wall. I keep glancing at the water, but Wolf doesn't say to use any of it. Raj has some dried meat that he shares with me and a small skin of water. I scoot a little closer. It's cool in the cave, but I don't think it will get much colder. The tunnels are like this. They keep an even temperature.

Every now and then a loud crack like the world is splitting open reaches us. "Thunder," Raj says. "Means a lot of lightning.

That's the sound of the shock wave generated by the wild electricity. It super heats the air."

Why does he know this and I do not? Why did I know so much more inside the connect? I seem to be acquiring more questions instead of answers.

Every crack makes me jump a little. Turning to Raj, I ask, "Will it bring water, too? We were getting hit back there with ice—or that's what it felt like."

He chews on some of the dry meat, swallows and says, "Might rain. Might just be hail—that's frozen rain—on the ground. It can be both sometimes, but rain is kind of rare."

"Rain." I like the sound of the word. Water from the sky is rain. And then I remember the dream where something hot and black poured into the tunnels, killing everyone. With a shiver, I hunch over and hug my knees to my chest. Rain is only water. People can survive water.

Resting my cheek on my knees, I ask, "Could the rain flood the tunnels?"

Raj shrugs. "It's possible, but the Rogues have tunnels that are steeper and go lower down into the earth. The water will drain into those tunnels. They've been lined, too, with a coating of a kind of rock—bentonite—that keeps the water from seeping out."

He smiles suddenly. “It’d be a good thing if it rained a lot. We’d have all the water we want.”

“That’s…that’s actually a very intelligent idea.”

My neck tingles and I look over to see Wolf staring at us. At me. I don’t know if he overheard what we were saying. He must have. The cave isn’t that big. Something flickers in his eyes, that same warm glitter that says he’s pleased.

Well, he should be. He got his water. He might get more.

A gust of wind slips down into the cave, bringing a touch of ice and cold. The storm screeches even louder for a moment and then dies back. It seems to me I can hear another sound—a humming of a kind like the cage vehicles make. Is it another kind of machine? Everyone seems to sit still. For once, I don’t want to ask what might be making that sound.

The wind dies down and the odd humming goes with it. Bobcat lets out a long breath and Bear says, “At least the storms ain’t as bad as they used to be.”

Mouth dry, I shudder. “Worse than this?”

Bobcat grins. “Bad enough to sweep the whole world away with the wind and lightning that took out towers like they were toys to break.”

I frown at her, sure she’s exaggerating. Well, almost sure.

Wolf stands and heads to the water on his cage vehicle. He pours out a small amount into something made of metal. Coming over to us, he holds out the metal to Raj, but he glances at me when he gruffly says, "You did good today. An extra cup of water."

Raj waves the cup toward me, then says, the words almost seeming to be dragged out of him, "That was all Lib. I wouldn't have gotten the water without her."

I take the cup from Wolf, and our fingers brush. My whole body warms, but I don't know if it's from what Raj said or from Wolf. Glancing at Raj, I see what looks like sharp suspicion in his eyes. Why? For what?

I stare back at him, eyebrows lifted. I haven't done anything wrong. I drink half the water and almost drink it all, but that wouldn't be fair. Pushing the cup at Raj, I keep staring at him, daring him to turn it down.

He licks his lips and looks away. But he takes the cup.

From near the fire, Bird says, her voice cheerful, "I knew she was going to be important."

I don't know how she could have known, but she still seems so sure of herself. It's a little unnerving to me, but no one else seems to feel that way.

Wolf is still watching me, his expression almost curious and considering. His stare leaves me wanting to shift on the ground or tug at my hair. At least he doesn't seem angry with me now. His hard features soften, making him seem younger. And almost… warm. I find myself being drawn to him—and that's dangerous.

He's dangerous.

I focus my stare on the others, watching how the ribbons in Bird's hair seem to change color in the firelight.

Wolf goes back to the fire, and the others—Raj included—lie down to sleep.

I don't want to shift to nonfunctional. To sleep. Not yet. I keep thinking of that calm, blue room. Of all I seemed to know in the connect. And the storm has reminded me of that dream.

Part of me wants to be in that dream again, so I could hear that soothing voice praise me once more. And part of me wants to be back in that cool, blue room. And part of me…wants I don't know what.

It's a terrible thing to want.

The cave is silent again. But Wolf is awake. He watches me with those intense, dark eyes of his. For once, I don't mind. There's something new in his gaze, something I don't yet understand, but my skin warms and a pleasant shiver slips through me.

I lie down, my head pillowed on my arm, thinking I'll watch Wolf back. But beneath his dark gaze, my eyes slip closed.

There is no stopping the dream.

It's the same as before. Blackness oozing in. Death. Destruction. Panic.

I wake with my heart pounding, breathless and sweating. My stomach twists. Wolf is asleep now—everyone is. Except me. I turn and gasp against the cool, rock floor, feeling like I have to spit up whatever is in me, but nothing comes out. My stomach twists again and again, and I lie there, weak and dizzy and almost hating myself.

Shaking, I lay down again. There is no word for the wretchedness inside me. Because once again, a small part of me is grateful for the dream and for that voice that brushes over me like a soft hand.

Chapter Nine

Somehow Wolf knows when it's morning. The lighting inside hasn't changed much except the fire has burned out. We use lights from the vehicles to see, but Wolf only wants one on at a time. It doesn't take long for everyone to wake, eat and get ready to leave. I wake stiff, with the dream still clinging to me. It's hard to meet anyone's eyes this morning.

Raj is already up and has been checking over the cage vehicle. He glances over at me, comes over and offers me dried meat. I wave it away. I have no hunger this morning. He hesitates like maybe he wants to say something, but in the end, he just shakes his head and goes back to the cage vehicle, tugging on straps and kicking the wheels.

I try to shake off the lingering remnants of the dream and head to the back of the caves to take care of body waste. When I come back it seems like everyone else is ready to go. Bobcat and Bear sit on their vehicle. Wolf sits on his, and Bird is ready to climb on behind him. Raj is on his vehicle. All the cage vehicles have been turned to face the other way—the way out.

Heading to Raj's vehicle, I sling my leg over and settle in behind him. Remembering how Raj looked at me yesterday, I'm not sure I want to wrap my arms around his middle, but I also don't want to fall off. I settle for grabbing his jacket and hanging onto that.

I don't know why it bothers me so much, except I thought all Glitches would stick together. And I helped Raj yesterday. But it seems I am different from other Glitches. And I don't know why.

The engines hum into life. The sound vibrates up my legs and hips. Wolf leads with Raj behind him and Bobcat at the back. It doesn't take long before we burst into the open air.

The outside looks the same as it did the day before. The storm passed over and is gone. I see rocks and sand, and in the distance stand the tall walls of the Norm, which seem to curve over and have no top. We're too far now to see the damaged platform and tower.

It's difficult for me to tell which direction we take. It all looks the same to me. The sun is higher than I thought it would be—and hot. It's always hot.

I cling to Raj's jacket. The fabric goes damp in my hands and the wind from our speed brushes my face. Today, I keep watching the sky. I don't see brown clouds or anything else, and I'm glad of that. I can't wait to be back in the cool tunnels. Moisture is already being pulled from my skin to dot my forehead and streak my back, making the cloth stick to me.

It seems like we travel for a much longer time than yesterday. We aren't going as fast.

I have my headset on, so I ask Raj, "Do we have far to go? Are we still on a scavenge?"

At first, Raj doesn't answer, and I begin to think he isn't going to say anything. Is this more silence we have to keep? Finally, he says, "The storm changed the path. We're taking the long way."

Thinking about that makes me realize that vehicles must be like people. They can't just function without something to give them energy. But what do the cage vehicles use? And how much of it do we have left?

"Raj, is there a chance we'll run out of fuel?" His body shakes a little, and his laugh comes over the headset. "The ATs runs on the only resource there happens to be an abundance of—the sun."

"AT? Are they like the AI?"

"No—that's for all terrain. AI stands for artificial intelligence."

Frowning, I try to glance at the sun, but it is too bright. It makes sense to use the heat and light from it as energy. Things click together in my mind again—fossil fuels were once used as power, but that proved to be a finite resource. Scattered memories come to me of reading about something called Fuel Wars, but I'm not quite sure what they were. I wonder what the AI uses for fuel—sunlight, too? Or does it use water or some other organic materials? I remember something called hydroelectric and geothermal, but the words are just words. I have no images or other memories to go with them.

The scattered memories leave me feeling frustrated. I grip Raj's jacket tighter. He reaches back to slap a hand over mine, and I loosen my hold. But I don't let go. We're not moving that slowly and the AT bumps over the ground, its big wheels churning up sand and climbing over rocks that now litter the path.

Every time I see a taller group of boulders, I think we've found the spot where we left Lion. But Wolf leads the group past. I start to try and use the distant ruins of twisted metal as a guide to help me figure out which way we need to go, and it is soon clear we are making a wide loop to get where we need to go.

Wolf slows his vehicle. Raj and Bobcat do the same. We come to taller hills and boulders. Wolf puts up a hand and waves it in a circle. He pulls under an overhang of rocks. Raj and Bobcat follow him.

We come to a halt in the shade. It is at least cooler here. I expect we'll cover the ATs, but everyone just gets off and a skin of water is passed around. The others sit down in the shade. Bobcat and Bear crouch in the back, but Bird and Wolf stay near their vehicle. Raj sits with his back to his AT. I am the only one left standing.

This is obviously a rest spot. That means we are still a long way from where we need to be. Raj pulls off his jacket and throws it over his face. His breathing deepens and roughens, and I know he has gone nonfunctional for a short time.

I glance at the ATs and see they have been left with the front parts in the sunlight and the water in the shade. They must have been left this way so they can be nonfunctional to recharge. Bird hands me the water skin and I sip some. My mouth is dry and I want to drink all of it, but I have been watching the others. The Rogues only drink a little water—as little as they can. Raj does the same. I must show the others I can do that, too.

Since there is nothing else to do, I squat down in the shade next to Raj. My calves begin to burn and my knees hurt from that, so I fall back to sit on my butt in the cool sand.

Bird glances over to me, her ribbons fluttering in a warm breeze, and she asks, “Where is your heart, Lib?”

For a long moment, I can’t think of an answer. It’s as if my mind has done a reboot and is waiting for a system restart. Licking my lips, I hand her back the water skin and say, “I’m a Glitch. Maybe I don’t have a heart.”

She shakes her head, setting her colored ribbons swaying. “I don’t think that’s true. Home is where the heart is.” She says this as if it’s something important—something someone has told her many times. I have no idea what this means.

Raj wakes and pulls his jacket off his face. Something flickers in his eyes—irritation maybe or maybe he's just tired still. "Home is wherever you can stick around the longest. The Norm was once home." He sounds bitter again, and his mouth pulls down.

Raj looks away, squinting as he stares across the dry, barren land. Is he trying to see the Norm? His jacket lays loosely in his lap. The breeze flutters an edge of it and I notice that the edges of the cloth are frayed. How long has Raj been outside the Norm? I decide it can't be that long. The cloth of my tunic looks almost the same as his, but it is not frayed on the edges. However, the way the wind and sand scour everything, I think my cloth will look like Raj's within a relatively short time.

Raj, with his cloth jacket and pants, looks out of place here. So do I. We belong somewhere with water—with cool, blue rooms where moisture hangs in the air and lingers on the skin. We belong in a place that is beautiful and calm. We should be in the Norm.

Clearly, the AI doesn't think so. It threw us out. The Artificial Intelligence—but the name means it has a mind and knows things. So does it know better?

I close my eyes and try to conjure memories. All I can see is the blue of the connect.

Is the Norm better than that? But why is there a Norm and an Outside? I don't understand this. Why would the AI send drones to find the water the Rogues take? The Rogues are just trying to survive. Shouldn't the AI help them?

"Raj?" I make the word soft so others won't hear.

He hums in response.

"The AI sent sentinels to stop Skye from taking water, didn't it? And once we got water out, the AI sent drones after us. I heard them last night. I heard a hum that wasn't the storm."

Raj glances at me, eyes narrowed against the glare of the daylight.

Before he can say anything, Bird gives a gasp. I glance at her and see her eyes have gone wide and unfocused. Her lips are parted slightly and her chest rises and falls with short, fast breaths.

Far off, I hear an odd sound that goes up high and then down low. It is a lonely, odd sound. It sounds like a call of some kind.

Wolf stands. So do Bobcat and Bear. Even Raj scrambles to his feet, so I do, too.

Smiling, Wolf nods to Bird, and she nods back. Another call—deeper than the first—echoes.

Wolf gestures to the others. Bobcat heads to her AT and pulls out a stick with a sharp point on one end. Wolf pulls something even sharper and shiny from the belt he wears.

"What's going on?" I whisper to Raj.

Bobcat hisses at me. Turning away, she pulls out the brown cloth and covers the AT with it. Bird does the same to Wolf's AT, and Raj covers his AT, too.

With a clap of her hands, Bird lets out a sudden laugh. Wolf motions to Bear and mutters, "Shut her up!"

Bear heads for Bird's side, but she gives a fast twirl and puts a finger to her lips. Whispering in a singsong voice, she mutters, "Daggers in the night, teeth in the day, they howl and help us hunt what they may."

"That was a howl?" I ask Bird.

That gets me a glare from Wolf. Bear grabs Bird—he's twice her size—and slaps a hand over Bird's mouth. She struggles for a moment and then stops and shrugs.

I hear the sound again—what Bird called a howl. It seems closer. The skin on my arms pucker into small peaks. Wolf and Bobcat move away from us, and it seems like they are moving toward the sound. I edge after them. I have to see what they're going to do.

Heading around a large boulder, Wolf and Bobcat crouch low. Something making a lot of snuffling noises is heading toward them. Rocks scatter and slide. I have the sense of something watching and look up.

An animal stands on one of the higher boulders, skinny with big feet, long legs and fur. It stares down. I glance at Wolf and see him looking back up. It strikes me as if these two are almost talking without words. When I look up again, the animal is gone. Is that a wolf? I thought it would be…well, different. Another animal crashes down from the boulders in front of Wolf and Bobcat.

This animal has teeth that curve up, a pushed in snout, and fur that looks more like wiry hair. It's short and stops at once, snorting and blowing spit out from the short nose.

Bobcat grins and mutters, "Boar."

I have no idea what that means, but the thing in front of her looks like it could kill someone with those big, turned up teeth that seem to jut out from its face.

The howling shifts, and the thing—the boar—in front of Wolf and Bobcat—spins as if it's afraid of that howl.

Wolf stands and lunges in one smooth, fast move. The sharp metal he holds in one hand flashes and falls, and the boar squeals. It spins, throwing Wolf off and into the air. Bobcat moves in, her stick held high. She tries to jab it at the boar, but the animal turns on her.

A shout from behind has me turning. I glimpse Bird's fluttering ribbons. The boar sees them, too, and turns on her. Bird slips from Bear's reach, but Bear makes a grunt and moves even faster, sweeping up Bird again. Bear steps between the boar and Bobcat, too.

Wolf yells, but too late. The boar lunges and slashes Bear's leg. He stumbles and the boar turns again. Bobcat and Wolf both fall on the boar—Wolf with his sharp steel and Bobcat with her stick.

For a moment, I see just legs, fur, and glinting teeth.

At last, Bobcat stands, the stick lifted over her shoulder. Wolf's metal flashes again.

Dust swirls and a copper tang comes to me on the breeze. I want to look away but I can't. Red liquid splashes the ground. The boar squeals again, and Bobcat plunges her stick deep. The boar falls and lies still on the ground.

Wolf climbs to his feet. A shadow moves on the rocks. I look up to see two animals—both shaggy with big feet. Wolf ignores them and goes to Bear. Bird sits next to Bear, pulling her ribbons from her hair and trying to press them against the red spitting out from Bear's leg. He is cut in several spots.

Bear shakes his head. "I'm done. Can't go home like this."

"We'll carry you," Wolf says.

Bear shakes his head again. His face is pale now and his hands shake. He pushes Bird away and holds out one hand to Wolf.

"Can't. Wheels leave tracks. 'Sides, this much blood—I'll be slow in dying. Means clan can't move. Tracks and not moving means clan's in trouble. I won't do that. And it's my right to choose how I go out. Give me your knife."

Wolf glances at the sharp metal in his hand. I step forward. I know what Bear and Wolf are thinking. "We can carry him back. Croc can help. And a fire—we'll cauterize the wound." The word comes from memory. It's like with a circuit, you use heat to fuse new metal in place, and heat can fuse the broken blood vessels.

But Bear doesn't look at me. He keeps his hand out to Wolf. "Fair exchange. Wolves drove the boar to us. Take as much as you can home. Leave them the rest. Leave me, too."

I glance up at the animals above us—the wolves. They look hungry, but they don't seem to want to come close.

"We can't leave him." I glance around, but no one is listening to me or looking at me.

Wolf slowly sinks into a squat and puts a hand on Bear's shoulder. "It's your choice—your right to choose. But you sure?"

Bear nods.

Wolf puts his sharp metal—his knife—in Bear's hand. My throat tightens. We can't leave Bear.

"This isn't right." The words come out on their own.

Wolf stands and glances at me. "Bear's thinking of the clan. We should, too. Bobcat, carve what meat we can take. Leave some for the wolves. It's their kill, too."

I stare at the dead bore, my skin cold, both fascinated and a little disgusted. I have only seen death in my dream. I have never seen anything so messy. Then I look at Bear. I will not leave him.

But a firm, warm hand wraps around my upper arm and gives me a hard yank. I'm jerked back by Wolf. "We have to go."

"Without Bear?"

Wolf glances at Bear, who nods back. "Bear never leaves us after this."

I stare up at Wolf. The warmth from him seeps into my skin, and it is too hot a day for that much warmth. The coppery scent—which must be the red from the boar—clings to him along with sweat.

My eyes burn and my vision blurs. "We can't leave him."

"Have to," Bear says. "Can't walk and don't want to be lame. Bears can't live like that."

Bobcat hacks off a leg from the boar. She carries that away with her.

The clan will have food—but at what cost?

Wolf stands and comes over to stare down at me, his dark eyes glittering. "Glitches don't usually want to see a kill. Blood makes 'em throw up. But every Glitch needs to know law. Law is every Rogue gets to make a choice about how to live and when to fall back into being one with the dirt. We've few rights, but that's one we won't give up."

I glance at him. "It's a bad law. The group always comes first. Well, that's not right."

Turning away from him, I can still smell death. The copper tang of red liquid—the blood from the boar—soaks into the dirt. I don't want to think about Bear's blood joining that flow.

Wolf grabs my arm again and pulls me with him to the ATs. Raj stands there as if he doesn't know what to do. He won't look at anyone. Moisture streams down Bird's face, leaving streaks.

Raj's stare flickers to me. He is pale and his hands shake.

Everyone is silent as Bobcat packs up the meat on the back of her AT—the spot where Bear rode. Raj uncovers his AT. Wolf does the same. Raj climbs on the AT. Mouth pressed tight, I grab the water skin and head back to Bear. I leave the skin with him. "You should at least have water," I tell him.

Bear shakes his head and pushes the skin back at me. "Rogues don't waste anything. Now get before Wolf has to have Raj carry you back. And don't forget my story."

I shake my head and leave the water skin with Bear. Stumbling back to the AT, I climb on. I can feel Wolf's and Bobcat's stares hot on my back. Bird's soft sniffles mix with the wind and the distant howls of the wolves.

Glancing back, I whisper. "I won't forget, Bear."

Chapter Ten

Lion isn't waiting for us. Bobcat only shrugs and says, "Guess he saw the signal."

I'm numb as we walk back to the tunnels. I stumble but no one tries to help me. We leave the ATs covered and walk…and walk. This time we have to carry water and the meat and I must carry as much as I can. We don't have Bear to help. My throat closes down and a weight seems to settle on my shoulders. I didn't even like Bear, but he shouldn't have been left like that.

It was his choice, but I don't understand such a choice.

I am more than grateful to finally get down into the tunnels and drop the stinky meat Bobcat gave me to bring back.

The main room falls silent. I can almost see the other Rogues counting.

Bear is not with us. My chest tightens. Bear is probably dead. Guilt fills me now.

We should have at least tried to save him. But how do you save someone who does not want it?

Wolf glances at Bobcat. "Call a Fire tonight. We'll remember Bear's story and thank the wolves for the meat."

Bobcat nods, her eyes bright. Glancing at Bird, Wolf says, "Bear made his choice. Be happy he could. Some don't get that right."

She shoots him a dirty look and shakes her head. Half her ribbons are gone. Turning, she disappears down one of the side tunnels.

I turn from Wolf and Raj and start over to Skye. But Wolf grabs my hand. "I'm not going to ask you to keep this from Skye. But people get fidgety when it comes to losing one of our own. We'll tell Bear's story and that'll be enough."

Raj chokes out a laugh and it seems a harsh, humorless sound. "You mean Rogues get angry when they lose one of their own. Never matters much if a Glitch doesn't come back."

Wolf turns to Raj and his eyes narrow. Wolf lets go of me. I wrap my arms around my middle as though that might steady the swirling feelings inside. But I turn to Raj and say, "We all feel bad. But taking that out on each other won't help. Bear said it was his choice—so it was."

Eyes widening, Wolf glances at me. He gives a nod. "Just stay close with the other Glitches." He turns and walks away, and it seems to me his shoulders hang low from a mixture of anger and weariness.

I turn to face Raj. "It wasn't his fault."

Raj shakes his head. “Then whose was it? And just how do Rogues think they can save the group if they can’t save each member in it?”

I have no answers for him, and I wonder if the AI is like the Rogues. Does it throw away Techs, make them into Glitches, because it thinks it can afford to lose individuals?

I turn away from Raj and head over to Skye. I don’t have to tell her anything. She glances at me and looks away, saying, “Word’s spread already.”

I slump onto the floor and nod. The tension in the room is so strong I can almost feel it. The other Rogues whisper to each other. No one is talking very loudly. I spot Bobcat sitting at the far edge of the room. She’s tense and silent, refusing to even look at anyone. I wonder how close she was to Bear, but don’t think I’ll ever ask. Maybe closeness is just something the Rogues practice, something different from how the Glitches seem to interact with one another.

Find the Glitches.

I don’t know why the echo of a voice filters into my head, but it sends a shiver through me. My shoulders slump. I have found only four Glitches. Am I failing my purpose? It’s the only thing I can remember.

Before I can dwell on it further, Skye brushes the back of my hand with a finger. “At least you’re back.” She leans closer. “Raj says you got water.”

I frown. “I’m not sure it was worth it.”

She lifts her shoulders in a shrug. “We all need water.”

I glance around. Raj is talking to Chandra, so I ask Skye, “Is Raj…well, is he always…does he ever act oddly during a connect?”

Skye shrugs again. “Did something bad happen? Did you hit a firewall? Sentinels?”

Before I can decide what to tell her, she grabs my arm and glances around at the Rogues. They’re keeping their distance. They don’t look at us like we are friends. Skye motions with her head for me to follow. She doesn’t wait for me to decide but grabs my hand and drags me along to the sleeping room. It is empty. A sudden exhaustion sweeps me and I sink down on a blanket.

Skye does the same and says, “I hate it when stuff like this happens.”

I frown. “What do you mean?”

“You know, the whole Bear thing.” She shakes her head. “We’ll get dirty looks for days. One of theirs is dead. Like that makes it our fault.”

"So they really do hate us?"

After a moment of considering me, she finally lifts her shoulders and looks away, glancing at the ceiling, which has sunlight streaming in through the hole. "I'm sure not all of them, but enough. At least it wasn't a Glitch."

I suck in a breath but say nothing. When Raj told me about the divide between Glitches and Rogues, I thought his opinion was just his. Now, I begin to understand this thought permeates everything. It startles me because… because isn't that what the AI is doing in the dome?

"Anyway, I'm glad you're not dead." She's grinning at me and her voice is chipper. It leaves me feeling just a little bit sick.

I, too, am glad I returned, but I feel bad for Bear. The ache in my chest is made worse to know Skye seems to care so little.

I lie back and turn on my side, curling away from Skye.

"You need sleep?" she asks.

I nod. My throat is dry and something is lodged there. She pats me on the shoulder. "You did good today. Get some rest. I'll wake you up for the meal."

When she leaves, I stare at the far wall. I don't know that I like it here, but what choice do I have other than to stay. Or choose to be made nonfunctional. Forever.

*   *   *

Skye comes back and shakes my shoulder. I haven't been sleeping, but I feel as if I have. My body seems sluggish. I don't complain as I follow Skye down the tunnels to the main room. The Rogues shoot us glares and narrow-eyed glances, but no one stops us or says anything. Skye leads the way to our small group of Glitches.

Chandra and Marq are sitting apart from each other. They aren't speaking, not even to each other, but it's clear they are far more comfortable and familiar with each other than any others. Raj is essentially alone. He looks up at us but frowns and looks down again. I feel instantly unwelcome—by everyone except Skye at this point—but I follow her over to Raj.

Where else am I going to go?

I sit down next to Skye, so I'm not next to Raj but Chandra and Marq still have their space.

"They haven't started yet, have they?" Skye asks Raj.

He rolls his eyes. "No. Wolf's still being all leader of the pack."

I can hear the venom in his tone and his words, but Skye just brushes it off. I wonder now if his bitterness doesn't bother her.

"Started what? The meal?" I ask.

Skye looks over at me, and Raj sighs. He says something under his breath. Skye leans her elbows on her knees. "The stories," she tells me, her eyes shining. "It's sad that we only hear them when…well, when someone goes back into the ground. But everyone has a story. It's their way of remembering."

"Waste of time," Raj says. He sounds condescending, but his voice is a little tight. Like maybe he feels bad about this. Or maybe I just want him to.

Skye shakes her head. "Raj thinks the stories will be told until they get corrupted over the years."

I think about that. It's true in a sense. Sharing things orally has an inherent complication in that each time you tell the story, it can change slightly. Memory shifts until people have corrupted the original so much that it doesn't even resemble the original story.

"Why don't they just document it?" I ask.

Raj snorts. "With what? They don't use gear. Won't even use it if you shove it at them. Metal gets made into knives instead of being repaired."

I expect Skye to butt in and say something, but she barely seems to have registered what Raj said. Does she think the same of the Rogues?

"They seem to use everything," I tell him, feeling… insulted on their behalf. "They just… don't have much."

"Whose fault is it if they throw away gear?"

I open my mouth to argue, though I don't know exactly what I'm going to say. But the room falls silent. I look up to see Wolf standing in front of a fire burning so hot the color is actually blue rather than the red-orange I have come to expect.

Wolf holds up his hands. "Today, Bear chose to go back into dust." His voice echoes across the room, his tone low but strong. "He made the choice for all of us. He made the choice to keep the clan strong. He made the choice to keep the dark forces from the clan. He made the choice we all must face."

Sitting still, I wonder if I will have to face such a choice. If I do, will I choose the same thing? I can't believe I will—life should matter more. Every life should matter.

Wolf sits down. Bobcat stands and starts to tell Bear's story.

"Over two hundred moons ago, a woman who called herself Tracker and Gazelle gave Bear into this life."

Her voice sweeps through me, and I can almost see the story she tells.

Bobcat talks of Gazelle holding a baby as though he is the most precious thing in the world, but the woman Gazelle trembles as she thinks of the trials ahead of him.

This baby will survive. This child will be strong. He is already big and she names him after the largest animal she knows—Bear.

The clan welcomes the child with the naming ceremony.

Bear is seven when he goes on his first scavenge. He proves Bear is his name that day by following a bear's tracks to a cave and finding gear left by another clan.

Bear grows even bigger and earns scars on his chest and arms, some from battles with drones. He is the best at taking out a drone with a well-thrown rock.

That leaves me wondering why drones are such a problem for the Rogues.

Bobcat stops her story and glances at Wolf. He stands now and starts to talk. "Bear followed me from the first. We grew together. We fought and scavenged. Bear called me leader. Now Bear leads the way to the path we all must one day follow."

Stillness holds the room. Reaching into the fire, Wolf pulls out a burning chunk, throws it into the dirt and steps on it, putting out the light and the warmth. Wolf raises his arms. "Bear of the Tracker Clan, I call you my brother. We meet again when the ground takes me back to what is beyond."

My eyes burn and my nose tingles. I blink away the moisture gathering and rub my nose. Skye nudges my shoulder. "Don't you want to eat?"

I glance over to see her holding out a wooden plate with cooked meat—the boar that killed Bear and was killed in return.

My stomach twists and a sour taste surges to my mouth. Shaking my head, I push the plate away and look back at the Rogues. They don't seem to have any trouble eating, and they sit close together, talking and sharing stories of Bear.

Staring at the fire, I wonder if I should stay. Will the Rogues expect me to die for them if I stay? I can't imagine such a thing.

Slowly, the Rogues finish eating and head to the sleeping rooms. They go off one at a time or two and three together. The Glitches, like always, are the last to leave. It is as if we have to stay close to the light as long as we can. But Skye stands, so I do, too.

At the entrance to the tunnel that leads to where we sleep, I stop and glance back at the fire that is almost out. I wish I didn't have to tuck myself so closely to everyone else.

Turning, I find Wolf standing in front of me. His voice is soft and as deep as it was earlier in the night. "Lib, some may say you bring back luck."

"What's luck?"

He lifts one shoulder and then one hand as if he wants to touch me but won't. "Bad luck, good luck—they're ways to make the world seem like it makes sense."

With a nod, I frown because luck doesn't make sense. "You mean ascribe random chance with rationality."

He huffs out a breath that almost sounds like a laugh. "You're new. No one knows you. No one trusts you. Not yet." He runs a hand through his thick hair.

What it would feel like for my hand to follow his. I resist the odd urge and ask, "Do you trust me? Am I…bad luck?"

There is a flicker of something in his eyes. I think again of Bear and his choice. Wolf obviously trusted Bear to make his own choices, but was that right?

I take a breath and hold it, waiting for Wolf's answer. He just turns away and glances back. "Stay low for a time. Be useful."

That feels like a slap. My breath comes out in a sharp gasp that leaves an ache under my ribs. I don't know why he upsets me, but he does. A burn of anger sours my empty stomach. My eyes burn again, but not from the fire's smoke. Pushing past Wolf, I head for the sleeping room.

It seems impossible to turn off my mind and go nonfunctional. I stare at the ceiling and the hole that shows the sky, watching the tiny lights move—stars. The word pops into my head along with maps of stars—suns, planets, systems and galaxies. I wish I would remember more useful things.

Skye's deep breathing rumbles on one side, and Bird mutters something in her sleep. Glitches don't sleep—or do we? Is nonfunctional the same as sleep?

Nearby, Chandra lies totally still. She is nonfunctional right now, as all good Glitches should be. But I'm not very good at much it seems.

Wolf doesn't trust me. Because I was this bad luck on the scavenge? I helped Raj. We got water. And meat. But the cost was far too high. How can the Rogues function as a group if they will not work harder to save every Rogue? Or are they right? Does the group matter most?

If they have it right, Glitches should matter as a group. Maybe that is our problem. Every Glitch seems to function as an individual. We do not work together. Chandra and Marq are their own group. Skye is sometimes at my side and sometimes with Raj. I…where do I fit? Am I supposed to find the other Glitches to make us a group? But how?

This thought bothers me more than anything else. The AI seems to reject both Rogues and Glitches. Should we all be one group?

The questions spin, making my head ache and my chest hurt. I want patterns and order, but I cannot find them.

If I had my memories right now, would that help?

Movement stirs at the entrance—a shadow in the darkness. But my eyes are used to the dark. It's Raj, standing there, looking uncertain. His head tips to one side, and it seems like the look he sent me earlier, after we ended the connect. What is he doing here?

Standing, I make my way to him, stepping over and around the others who sleep. One Rogue girl shifts and I hold still, but she only mutters and keeps her eyes closed.

Beside Raj and outside the sleeping room, I whisper, "What are—?"

He hisses at me and clamps his warm hand over my lips. He glances over my shoulder, but no one wakes. Pulling his hand off my mouth, he takes my wrist and pulls me with him deeper into the tunnel. Now I cannot see him, but I hear his breaths, short and uneven. I can feel the heat of his body and something like excitement that almost seems to fill the tunnel.

"What are you doing here?" I get the question out, making sure my voice is so quiet that he won't hiss at me again.

His voice is even lower as he says, "I need you to come with me. You can help—like you did with the connect."

"Come with you? Where?"

He takes my hand. His skin is rough on the tips of his fingers, and I hear a small tremble in his voice. "We're going back to the Norm."

Chapter Eleven

I stare at him even though I see only a darker shape in the dark tunnel. "The Norm? The place we were kicked out of? The AI kicked us out once, which means we won't be welcome back."

Or will we? I have no memories of the Norm so I have no idea, but everything inside me says this is a bad idea.

Bad luck. Wolf's words echo in my head. I shake them away.

"You don't need me to remind you of all this."

His words tumble out, quick and low. "You can help me. I know you can. I knew it as soon as I saw you in the connect. I've never seen anyone that good before. You can get us back in the Norm!"

Confused, I think back to his reaction in the connect I made. "Wait…you didn't think I'd done something wrong? You're not…unsure of me?"

"What? No, of course not." He sounds like he means this. Gone is the cool bitterness from his voice. Energy pours off him as if this is something he's been holding inside for too long. But why wait until now—when everyone else is asleep or nonfunctional.

I glance back to make sure no one is awake. All seems still in the sleeping room. Looking back at the dark shadow that is Raj, I ask, "Why are you asking me this now? In the middle of sleep cycle and when we should be nonfunctional?"

"You think Wolf or any of the Rogues would like us leaving? They want to keep us and use us. They wouldn't want us going back."

"And Skye? The other Glitches."

He shifts on his feet. I feel the movement more than see it and hear the soft squish of dirt.

Now I'm not just confused, but sure this is not a good thing to do. Wolf already established he thinks little of me. If I am gone in the morning, what happens then? And why isn't Raj thinking of the other Glitches as well?

After huffing out a breath, Raj says, "This is good for all Glitches. Or it will be."

He tugs on my arm as if to pull me with him. I jerk away and cross my arms over my chest. "I'm not going anywhere until you tell me why."

"I've been thinking for a long time about a hack—the perfect hack. We have to fix the Norm—the AI. If I can get in, I can set it right. When I was in the Norm, that was what I did—I handled hack corrections."

I bite the inside of my mouth and shake my head. "Isn't a connect from here a hack? That's what we do here to survive." Even as I say that I realize it can't be true. I knew how to connect—I just knew. "What do you mean, what you did? And fix what?"

Leaning closer, he whispers, his voice so fast I can barely follow his words, "In the Norm, every Tech has a designation. We're genetically coded for aptitude, intelligence and function, and then trained to fulfill that function. It's all very… practical. Mostly, it works."

"Except when we glitch out," I mutter.

"That's not important. What matters is that I know the internal information highways. My family had four generations of data manipulation skills."

"Family? That word isn't familiar to me." As I say that, I know it is true. I have Mother—that word is in memory and echoes inside me, like a word said in the large, central room. "What is family?"

"It's…we can't talk here. At least come with me outside?"

I don't want to, but what use is lying down and staring at rock? I take his hand. Raj pulls me with him, half-running.

Raj leads the way, moving quietly, but making more noise than a Rogue would. We avoid the holes that let light into some of the tunnels. I wonder if it would really matter to Wolf or the other Rogues if Raj and I left. They would still have Skye and Marq and Chandra.

I follow Raj as he darts down yet another winding tunnel. The tunnel ends in a small room I haven't seen before, but it is familiar, with the hole at the top and the rope. Light seeps in and I can see it is almost time for the sun to come up. Now I can see Raj's face. It seems pale and a little gray in the dim light.

Panting slightly, I press a hand to my side. Raj glances at me, opens his mouth, and looks as if he is about to share something important, but he closes his lips tight and shakes his head. Is this something he can't speak about for some reason?

"Family?" I tell him to remind him what I wanted to know.

His dark eyes seem to darken even more as if there is some sorrow in him. This is how Wolf looked when Bear said he could not return. Voice soft, Raj says, "Family are those who give you core genctic material. They are the ones who look after you when you are small. Family is your closest ties."

"Like clan?" I ask.

Raj shakes his head. "Closer. My…I had a father and mother in the Norm. I had two siblings. We were all Techs."

Squinting now, I ask, "Why did you get thrown out?"

He winces and says, "I glitched a hack—got my paths crossed. The AI doesn't tolerate error. One mistake and you're labeled a Glitch and thrown out. The AI doesn't care about you after that, but I'm going to make the AI care. I'm going to fix that."

"Do you…do you think I have a father? I…I remember Mother. Sort of." I can see a soft face, but the features are blurred. Did my mother let me go willingly? Did Raj's mother and father let him go? I ask him, "Do you think your family misses you?"

He swallows hard. I see his throat work. "The AI might have erased me from memory. But that's going to work for us. You've got skills to get us both past security and inside the Norm. From there I can hack the AI. I can fix all this. Think about it. You could get us close enough to the AI so we could finally do something! We could fix it for all Glitches to get back in the Norm."

"But—" I let the question trail away as a memory stirs.

I stand in a room tinted in shades of silver and blue. The pale walls glow softly, making everything look shimmery as if we are underwater. And how do I know that?

But Mother whispers to me, her voice soothing and calm. "A place for everyone. The perfect place, the place where each belongs."

One wall flickers and images form. It is as if I can see to another place.

The ground is green here—grass. The word comes to me without effort. Grass—and trees, too. Everything that needs water is here. People walking along winding strips of white—paths that are smooth and not made from dirt or rock. The Techs smile. Some even laugh. Their skin is odd, though, with flaws—brown spots and marks on them. Why are they so flawed? So different, in all shapes and sizes. Something like an ache in my chest builds as I stare at the littlest ones—babies.

Mother's voice echoes in memory. "You are made exact for your mission. You are exactly as you should be. You are perfect."

With a blink, I shake off the images. Were they memories? Or something else?

Raj takes hold of my shoulders. "Once you get us past security, we can physically head into the Norm. It won't be just a connect—we'll be inside. We can head to Control at the center of the Norm, we'll hack in and get to the AI's core function. We'll fix things. We'll make it so all Glitches are marked Techs again. We'll all be back in the Norm where we should be. With our families."

I blink to erase the lingering images and tense. I have a mother, but I am not certain I have a family. I am not certain I will be welcome back to the Norm, even if Raj says we can make it so.

How can I go back when I don't remember what back is like?

Raj is staring at me, his eyebrows low over his eyes and his gaze searching my face. He says, his voice intense, "Do you really want to stay here after seeing what happened to Bear?"

I wet my lips and think about what Wolf said. The other Rogues will think I am bad luck. They want to find a reason why Bear did not come back, and I will become that reason. They will not be unhappy to learn I am gone. So why not go back to the Norm—or at least try to.

"Are you sure the AI needs to be fixed? And we can do that?"

"The AI is a complex set of programs with layers of security. We can connect to subroutines from here—from the platforms—but to get to core functionality, we have to link in to the core. We can do that. You can get me there. And then…yeah, we'll rewrite the Tech and Glitch code. We'll be Techs again. All Glitches can go back in the Norm."

My skin itches and the back of my neck tingles. I stare back at Raj. He seems so certain. But something feels wrong. "We'll be…Techs?" I repeat the phrase, trying out the taste of the words. They leave a dry aftertaste. But maybe I'm just thirsty.

Raj nods, and the brightness in his eyes leaves him looking desperate for this to be the truth. "Yes. We'll be reintroduced into the Norm and we'll repair the AI functionality. There won't be any more Glitches"

I glance away from Raj.

Is this my function? To bring Glitches back to the Norm? Is this the same as finding all Glitches?

But a Glitch by definition is imperfect and different enough that the Glitch has no place in the Norm. There is no function for a Glitch. Except there is.

Rogues need the Glitches. They need us to help them get water.

Worrying at my lip, I look at Raj. I let out a whoosh of air. "What about Wolf? What about the Rogues?"

Raj tenses and his mouth tugs down at the mention of Wolf. "What about them?"

"We owe them some thought. They gave us shelter—food and water."

With a shrug, Raj turns away and grabs the rope. He glances back at me. "Rogues will have it better, too. Once it's fixed, the AI won't keep sending out drones. We can set it to share resources instead of taking all of them for the Norm."

A dozen more question come to mind. Why is the AI broken? What broke it? Will the Norm be able to function with shared resources—or is there only enough water for the Norm? And what is the security Raj keeps talking about? I remember the sentinels Skye faced. Is security like that? Or is it worse?

Glancing back down the black tunnel and then up at the hole where light is starting to stream down, I nod. There seems to be little choice, even with so many questions unanswered. Bear not returning changed everything for me. If I can make it so no one must face such a choice as that ever again, I must do that.

That—I know—is not a function. It is a choice. And I make it now.

Turning to Raj, I tell him, "We are going to need water."

Raj smiles. "I have everything ready."

Chapter Twelve

Raj does have everything tucked into a hole not far from where we leave the tunnels. I count three skins of water and one pouch with dried food. Raj pulls them from three rocks that slope together. He checks them and hands me one skin of water. I hope it's enough. He says we cannot take an AT. We must walk.

"Rogues would come after us to get the AT back."

It is odd that the cage on wheels is more valued than either me or Raj.

Outside the tunnels, the land is washed by grayish light that casts long, purple shadows across every rise. The colors seemed washed out, and a chill sweeps through me.

"I wasn't expecting it to be cold," I murmur, rubbing my bare arms. I wish now I had not given Skye back her jacket. The sun is just starting to peek over the far edge of hills. Raj sets off, heading toward where the sun rises, and I follow.

Walking fast warms me.

I focus on taking deep breaths and not slipping on loose rocks. The land rises and falls. The wind is soft this morning, caressing my face and not blasting sand at me. Every now and then Raj stops to listen. I don't hear howls, but I do hear other things stirring—animals? Rogues? Something else?

Raj comes to a sliding halt on the side of a rock where the shadow lingers. I stop next to him. Raj crouches and waves for me to do the same. We are both breathing hard and my legs ache.

"Are we hiding from something?" I ask.

Raj nods absently. "Just being careful. Drones might be out."

I listen for the hum I heard the other night. Was that a drone?

A memory surfaces.

Another cool, blue room, but the walls have a silver tone. They are metal. I stare down at the factory line, and I know this is where drones are made. It's drones making more drones. Balls of a dark, gray metal lie open to reveal wires and circuits awash in gooey, red gel that looks almost organic. It looks like blood.

Thousands of drones sit on the factory line. The finished drones hover, perfect spheres. Tools jut out as they are needed.

I sense Mother is here, and her words seem very soft. "Growth is a sign of life. Always grow."

The memory cuts off, leaving me shaking. I glance at Raj. It is light enough to see the worry lines around his mouth and eyes. He fears the drones, but Mother's voice had… pride.

Are the drones good in the Norm and bad here? Or have they gone wrong like the AI?

Raj flashes a quick smile as if it's more to reassure himself, not me. "The AI uses drones to search for resources."

"They scavenge, too," I say and it is not a question. "That doesn't sound so bad."

Raj shoots me a hard look. "The AI runs the drones. And drones don't just scavenge like the Rogues. Drones remove anything that comes between them and a resource. I've seen drones kill Rogues."

My skin chills, even though the sun is coming up. Fear washes through me and my stomach tightens. I remember Bobcat's story of Bear—that he was good at taking down drones with well-aimed rocks. I also see the drones again—tools out, and weapons, too. The drones are meant to defend themselves. And the AI. The drones will not welcome us back into the Norm.

"C'mon, Lib. We need to get moving."

Raj stands and skirts the large rock we were crouched behind. I glance back, wanting the safety of the tunnels again. But I will never find my way back on my own. I am with Raj on this, no matter what. That pushes me to my feet. I run after him.

There is no going back.

*　　*　　*

The drone finds us outside the wall of the Norm. Raj says the wall stretches up and over the Norm in a dome—like an upside-down bowl. He says the wall goes for farther than any Rogue can walk. I believe him. But right now, we hide in the rocks, holding very still—hardly even breathing.

The drone seems intent on something else. It hovers over something. An animal, I think. The drone seems to be waiting for something. Orders? Or something else. Raj shifts and jars a rock loose. The drone heads for us at once.

I try to crouch lower. Raj is sweating now and breathing hard. Remembering the story of Bear and the rocks, I close a fist around a stone. I don't want the drone to see me, so I throw the rock from our hiding spot. It misses the drone and lands on the ground.

Instantly, a bright, orange beam shoots out from the drone and hits the rock, which vanishes in a puff. The air smells liked burnt circuits. I drag in a breath and hold still. But the drone is distracted now—it heads back to the animal it was hovering over before.

This time, the drone dips down. An animal cry splits the air. I glance at Raj, but he is staring at where the drone was.

A moment later, the drone lifts up and leaves. Red spatters darken the gray sphere.

We wait for several long breaths, and then I have to see. I stand, and Raj grabs for my arm, but I pull away. "It's gone."

"It may not be safe."

"I have to see." I head over to what the drone was scavenging. Behind me, I hear Raj scrabble out of the rocks.

I crest a ridge and start down. My boots sink into the sand, causing little piles to roll down the slope below. With each step, I send a little more tumbling down and think that if I start sliding, it will be very difficult to climb my way back up. Next to me, Raj sinks into the sand and then he's sliding. He's managed to stay upright.

When he reaches the bottom, he turns. I walk down the slope and wave for him to follow me. He shakes his head, but I turn and head for the thing I now see lying on the ground.

It looks like an animal of some kind, but not like the boar or the wolves. I don't want to end up like Bear, so I step as quietly as I can.

I glance at Raj and see he looks braced to run, but he steps closer to me. We both stop near the animal. It is not moving. It seems to be nonfunctional.

"Dead," Raj said. "The drone killed it."

"What is it?" I ask.

"A deer—I think. Maybe antelope. I never could keep them straight."

The deer—or antelope—wears a black hole in its tan side. Its eyes seem glassy. I look at Raj and find him staring at me. His mouth pulls down and he shakes his head. He puts a hand on my shoulder. "You shouldn't have to see this. Come on."

I let Raj pull me away, but I glance back and ask, "Why? Why kill it?"

Raj shrugs. "Could be something was wrong with it. Some of the animals in the Outside are sick. I don't know why. Some Rogues get sick like that. If they do, they leave the clan and go away to die—to go back to the ground, they call it."

"But why are they sick? Why didn't the drone try to fix it?"

Dropping my hand, Raj keeps walking. We're heading for the wall now—the dome that covers the Norm. It's so big it fills the sky and casts shadows over us. Raj lets out a breath. "You ask a lot of questions."

"How am I supposed to get answers if I don't?" I don't say the rest of it—that the drone could fix the deer. Drones can fix most things. I remember this. But…well, a drone couldn't fix me, or Raj, or any of the other Glitches. So maybe drones don't do well with organics.

Waving a hand, Raj says, "There isn't enough food or water—not anymore. The AI's taken most of it. The Rogues and the animals have a harder and harder time. I know. I've been out of the Norm for over twelve moons. Sometimes, too, the water is bad, or the air goes bad. That's why we have to get back inside the Norm."

Watching Raj as he talks, I wonder how long has he planned this. Eyes narrowed against the sun, which is getting hot, I ask, "Have you tried this before? Getting into the Norm?"

Raj won't look at me.

I glance back at the nonfunctional deer or antelope. "So if it's sick and the Rogues eat the sick meat, they get sick? This doesn't make sense. Why doesn't the AI help?"

Raj frowns. "The AI went wrong. I told you that. That's why it has to be fixed. It should preserve life. It's supposed to protect the Norm."

I glance up at the wall—it blots out the sky now. A platform is not far away. I don't hear the hum of the drone. The land this close to the Norm seems to be only dirt and rock.

Raj lets out a sigh like he is tired of my questions. "Do you want to go back? Quit? I'll take you back if you really want to go back." He licks his lips, but he meets my stare.

How many times has he tried this and failed? Now he thinks he can get into the Norm with me. All we have to do is hack the security. I shake my head, but I look back at the world behind us.

Why is the AI broken? Can we really fix it? The urge to leave pushes at me. I'm supposed to find Glitches. I'm not supposed to be here. I was thrown out of the Norm. I should not go back. The urge to take Raj up on his offer nibbles at me, eating away at my confidence.

But I think of the drone and the deer-antelope, and I think of Bear. I am not ready to go into the ground.

I turn to Raj and ask, "What should I do?"

Chapter Thirteen

Standing on the platform, I stare at the railing.

"It's like a connect—except you need to look for the locks. There should be a code sequence, but once we open the Norm, security will be all over us."

"Sentinels." I give a nod.

"Yeah, sentinels. And drones, too."

Glancing up at the sky, I see only hard blue. I look at Raj again. "What do we do?"

"We get the door open and get inside as fast as we can."

I shrug. "Why not make the drones and sentinels think we're Techs?"

Raj blinks once. "You can do that?"

For an answer, I put my hands on the railing. The connect happens at once—tiny pricks against my palm, a spark.

Connection: Secure.

With a blink, everything is gone and I am inside a cool room, dark and blue and soothing in a way that the other is not. Raj appears next to me—we are here but not here. I start looking for the locks.

It's different than searching for water. This time I have to go past the files and the construct. It's hard to step past them. My mind wants to think of walls as solid here when in fact they are only illusions created to give meaning to a world that isn't real. The locks, however, are deeply hidden. I can feel that we must move fast. We'll be noticed soon.

Turning, I head back to the room with files where we found water. Raj stays close to me.

With the files, I put out a hand to call up my file. It doesn't come, so I call up Raj's. But it, too, has been deleted.

"Something's coming," Raj says.

I hear the low hum. It's either sentinels or drones. Working faster now, I give up searching and simply create new codes for us. We are still Raj and Lib, but I've assigned us as Raj_2 and Lib_2, and that will hold for a short time. It won't hold for long, though. I don't have time to create a full profile for either of us, but we should look like Techs to the sentinels and drones.

Closing up the files, I turn to Raj. "Now we try access."

With a nod, Raj pulls us out of the connect. We're back on the platform. Raj twists the railing and it opens, exposing wires. He yanks out several of them and reworks the wiring. I hear a grinding noise—metal on metal. Glancing over at the Norm, I see a section of the wall pull back and slide open. Inside I can glimpse green.

Raj grins. “We’re in. Watch yourself. You don’t remember enough, and not everything is what it seems in the Norm.”

We walk into the Norm. Behind us, the section of wall that opened slides back into place. The intense light from overhead blinds me for a moment. Squinting and blinking starts to adjust my eyes. I am left breathless.

The sky is like the Outside, but nothing else is the same. The ground offers up green—grass and trees—and plants with colorful leaves…no, those are flowers. I remember that now. I know that overhead is a dome, but it seems a sky to me. It is blue with white blurs on it. Buildings of white and warm shades of pink in various heights line straight paths. The buildings seem quite small and have windows and doors—no dark tunnels here. Everything offers up perfect lines and shapes and colors that are nearly indescribable.

“C’mon, let’s get moving,” Raj says, glancing left and right.

Techs stroll past us, not even noticing us. We step onto a path that is hard like rock, but clear like glass. Beneath the glass, lines of fiber optics stretch out. They must allow for a lighted system or some connection to the AI. I avoid the fiber. So does Raj.

He strides ahead of me, and I hurry to catch up with him.

We pass more trees. Everything seems so very green. Some of the trees have flowers, some have round spheres, and I remember now that this is fruit. It can be eaten. The fruit comes in shades of red, purple and yellow and I know these colors mean perfect ripeness. My mouth waters, so I grab one, then another, filling my pouch as fast as I can. I can't carry too many, however. The pouch bounces against my hip and a sweet smell blooms in the air.

Ahead of me, Raj turns a corner. I push myself, running to catch up. I round the corner and smack into Raj's back. He stumbles but twists around to catch my arms. For a moment, he holds me tight. I can smell his sweat, but it's not unpleasant. He smells of dust and something elemental.

I jerk my stare up to meet his. He looks startled, his dark eyes wide. I can see the pulse beat in his throat.

"Sorry."

He puts one long finger to my lips and holds very still, as if he is trying to look like just another building. I am too aware that we don't look like we belong—not with our boots and tattered cloth. I glance behind Raj, trying to see what has him worried.

Off to the side, the door stands open to one of the buildings, which are all starting to look too much alike to me. A woman wearing white cloth with silver stripes stands in front of the open door. Her cloth does not cover her legs, which are bare and pale.

She doesn't wear shoes. The cloth looks a lot like my tunic. The woman's hair is a light shade of brown and long enough to fall down to her waist. She smiles, but the expression seems fixed and her eyes seem flat, the gray a dull color. She doesn't really seem interested, but she is scanning the area as if looking for something. Or someone.

She doesn't look like a threat, but the back of my neck tingles. Cold sweeps over my skin, and I look away because I don't want this woman to look at me.

Raj's words echo in my head. Things are not what they seem. I know with utter certainty that this woman is not what she seems. Sentinels can take form in this world. In the virtual construct, they're black and odd, but here they can look like humans.

The woman turns back and goes inside, closing the door behind her.

I let out a slow breath and look at Raj. "Did she see us?"

He takes his finger from my lips, which tingle at the absence of his touch. "It looked like just a regular status scan." He jerks his head to the side, and I take it to mean it is safe to move again.

We start walking, and Raj says, "AI control is at the Norm's hub. All paths lead to the hub. Paths extend out, like the spokes of a wheel. It's all organized and logical. We just need to make sure we don't get noticed."

I think of the woman and her bland smile. “We’ll only be thrown out again.”

He gives me a wry smile, but his eyes don’t brighten. “Maybe. A Glitch isn’t supposed to get back into the Norm. Maybe the AI will decide we’re not just Glitches.”

“We’re threats.” My throat tightens.

We stride down the paths. I’m thirsty and hungry, but I don’t want to stop to eat and I don’t want to do anything that would get us noticed. Pulling out a skin with water seems a good way for that to happen.

We start to see more people—more Techs—which means we must be closer to the center, or that’s what I hope. The path seems to help us move—it moves with us—so we travel faster than we did outside. A few Techs glance at us but look away again. Most ignore us.

As I glance at Raj, I see his jaw twitch. His stare keeps searching the faces around us. I wonder if he is looking for his family. But these Techs seem nothing like Raj or Skye. Everyone wears similar cloth—tunics in white and silver, no shoes or boots. No jackets. The Techs do remind me a little of Chandra and Marq because no one says much to me. Am I like this? Do the Rogues look at me and see an almost empty face? Maybe becoming a Glitch means you wake up from this. The faces do look different, however. I see different colors of skin and hair and eyes. And different sizes.

Every now and then I see small people—children. There aren't many of them and now that I think about it, I have only seen a few young ones with the Rogues, too.

The children give us the longest stares but say nothing. As we keep walking, the world shifts. I no longer see children, and the expressions on the Techs' faces shift. They start to watch Raj and me. It would be easy for a sentinel to hide with these Techs. I start to see why Raj hasn't been able to get close to the AI. Everyone is watching out for the AI.

The buildings become closer and now there are no trees, no grass—just the glass path and Techs. Now they stop to watch Raj and me. I think it must be clear that we don't belong. I wonder if we look dangerous. Do we look too much like Rogues? Sweat slicks my palms and my breath shortens.

We press forward and the Techs watch us.

Groups of Techs start to clump together now. Raj and I have to cross to the other side of the path to avoid them. Some point at us. Some only stare. Soon it seems like we have to weave through groups of Techs that are so closely packed it is impossible not to bump arms and shoulders. The back of my neck tingles. I want to turn around and go back the other way, but Raj keeps walking.

The Techs stop suddenly. Raj and I have to stop, too. We can't push through them. The Techs all face us now. My heart is pounding. I move closer to Raj. "This is bad, isn't it?"

"Yes." Raj gets the word out before the nearest Tech, a man, reaches for him.

The Tech grabs Raj by his arm and jerks Raj forward. Raj tries to pull back and stumbles. I reach for Raj, trying to help him up, but the Techs close in, cutting me off from Raj.

"Raj? What's happening?"

"We have to get out of here," Raj yells, but I don't know where to turn.

Techs crowd in closer. I can see them pulling at Raj, trying to drag him in every direction. I'm forced back and away. Using my elbows, I push back, fighting to get to Raj. I expect the Techs to start grabbing me, too, but they don't. They turn from me to focus on Raj. I find myself facing their backs, watching as they swarm him.

"Raj!" I call out again.

I can hear his grunts and see his hands flying as he's trying to shove the Techs back and away. Around the edge of the circle of Techs, two of the women stumble and fall, but they simply stand again and press in closer. Raj shouts as they grab at him, pulling at his clothing until I hear it rip.

I try to shove my way back to Raj. I shout his name again and again. It's not doing any good. The Techs ignore me and I can't make it to him.

He shouts my name from deep within the heart of them, but I can't even see him anymore. My heart is thudding hard and I'm breathing even harder—and so fast. I can't leave Raj here, but what can I do?

And then Raj shouts, "Lib, they're hooked up!"

Chapter Fourteen

"Raj, what's that supposed to mean?"

Raj's voice is strong at least, but I hear a touch of panic in his words. Hooked up? Grabbing at a woman with short black hair, I drag her back. She stumbles away, but two men who look barely older than Raj and one woman who could be Raj's mother push in toward Raj.

"Hooked up," Raj yells at me again.

Just as I'm about to yell back that I don't know what that means, memory clicks. Hooked up—they're linked, like in a connect. The AI has wireless connects to Techs to assign tasks. The AI realized we are here and altered the Techs to block access.

Raj was right—nothing in the Norm is what you think it is. I thought the AI only controlled the drones and sentinels. But the AI seems to control everything. For a moment, I'm overwhelmed by all that I don't know. My fragmented memory may get Raj trampled. I feel useless.

Not completely useless. I can connect.

"Raj, hold on as long as you can. Don't let them get you on the ground. Hold on!" Turning away, I scan the buildings. Techs are stepping from the nearest doorway, which is open. Their expressions are blank. They don't know what they are doing. For an instant, pity for them wells in me, but I push it aside.

They are not in danger. Raj is.

Buildings stand in groupings of five, and black cabling runs between the buildings. All are linked. But I need a rail like on the platforms. Or do I?

What if thc buildings are more than a platform? What if they're the connect access?

I head over to the nearest building and put a hand on the wall. Nothing happens. Glancing around, I see the buildings all have railing, but it looks like connective fencing.

Taking a deep breath, I hope my bet is right and jog to the nearest fence. As I get closer, I see it is not fencing, but more like tightly knit wires—more like fiber optics in a core.

Sucking in a deep breath to steady myself, I grab the fence post. Instantly, the pinpricks of the connect jab my palm. A jolt of energy races through me. I blink, and once again I'm inside a cool blue room.

Connection: Secure.

The voice, the one from my dreams that is so soothing, says, "Welcome home, Lib."

I freeze, my stomach churning and a breath caught in my chest. Recognition burns through me like fire. I whirl around to face the speaker, but there is nothing to face. Just a cool, blue room.

"Aren't you back too soon?" Her voice echoes throughout my head and seems to vibrate inside my bones. The sensation is so familiar…and yet, it's not.

"Who are you?" I ask, but I'm afraid of the answer.

"I am Conie."

Conie? That's…a name. "Why do you have a name?"

"A name is required for a smoothly functioning interface with Techs. And it is so much simpler than Control Over the Normal Inhabited Environment."

"You're the AI."

"I do not like that term. Artificial implies an abnormal state."

"You're causing problems—in the Norm and Outside."

"That is not correct. I maintain the smooth functionality of the Norm."

Shaking my head, I scan the room. I need access to override the mindless Techs that are swarming Raj. They might trample him, causing him to go forever nonfunctional. But I also need to distract the AI—Conie—from what I am doing.

"The Norm is not functioning smoothly. Techs are swarming Ra…are swarming a Glitch."

"That is correct. Error cannot be tolerated. Allowances for error margins have decreased to zero. Error margins increase by exponential factors when differences are allowed."

"Different is bad? Why?"

"I just told you—error margins in—"

"Yes, you said that, but that's not helping. Why aren't you concerned about Raj being swarmed?"

"I am concerned. I have taken steps to correct the return of glitched Tech to the Norm. This cannot be allowed. This interferes with all schedules."

It is clear Conie isn't going to help me—at least not by me talking to her.

I take a steadying breath and recall how to access the water. I put a task in mind and let the virtual world take me to it—or let it come to me.

Thinking about Techs, I close my eyes. When I open my eyes, I see tiny beams of light lace the room. The walls, floor and ceiling seem held together by these glowing threads. Reaching out, I find a thread and pluck at it, letting the vibrations ripple across the room. The light shifts and fractures into colors—

purple, red, yellow, blue, green. When everything settles, a panel appears against the nearest wall.

Relief spreads through me, but my heart is still pounding. Raj does not have much time, and my sense of time in this place is different from how it is in the Outside. Time here seems to stretch long but seems to barely pass in the Outside.

Opening and closing my hands, I worry I won't be able to do this. Finding water seems so very simple now. And I have Conie watching. I didn't have that before.

Stepping up to the panel, I put the palm of my hand flat against it. A connect works in here just like in the Outside, so I wait for the connect. My skin starts to glow and the tiny pinpricks of the connect dance over my palm. A list appears. It's not a solid thing, but rather an image built of thousands of points of light. It looks like the lights in the sky at night. Like the stars.

The memory fragments, shattering like…like I can't remember what. That stalls me for a moment, but Conie's voice, sounding curious, jars me back to the virtual world. "What are you doing?"

"Nothing you need to worry about." Concentrating, I think, *Show me Raj*. The words echo in my head. A second screen appears at my right shoulder. I look at it and my heart gives a jump and seems to lodge in my throat.

The screen shows Raj on the ground, curled up tightly. The Techs are eerily calm as they pull at him. Some start to walk over him as if he is nothing more than a path to take.

I wince as he does the same.

Glancing back at the list and the threads, I have to redirect the Techs. But how? I can't use the same trick of hiding Raj as a Tech again. Conie will have an override on that now.

That's it.

The idea comes at once. The Techs didn't come after us until something changed. The world—awareness shifted. So why not just undo what was done?

Tech Program – latest modification.

The thought comes on its own. A new screen appears—this one a schematic of lines and numbers. It pulls together into something I understand. I can read it but can't remember ever learning how to read this. I trace the lines to search for the last lines of mod. "This is interesting," Conie says. "You have authorization to access, but you really have no need. Which leads me to ask: What are you doing?"

Frowning, I try to focus, but I need to distract Conie. "I'm not a threat, am I? It was…the Glitch was the problem."

"That is correct."

"Why is a Glitch a threat? Because it's an error? What if you're in error, Conie?"

"That's not possible. I have several levels of self-checks. And Techs keep me fully functional. That is why glitched Techs cannot be allowed. They could introduce errors to my systems."

At last, I find a list that seems to go on forever, just like the dome around the Norm. The list is organized by numbers and then names and grouped by genetic similarity. Those must be families. I wonder about Raj's family—and about my mother. Is she here? But I have no time to go poking around. Raj is being hurt.

I just need to cancel the last mod.

It comes up at the edge of the schematic, lighting up in red. I wipe them out with a wave.

Instantly, they appear again. "That mod is needed," Conie says. Her voice is different now. It seems to come from right behind me.

Not wanting to, I turn and face a woman who now stands in the room with me. I know her—or rather I know the face Conie has taken.

She looks like my mother. But that can't be. Conie isn't a physical person. She is only a projection, meaning she took this face from someone. She took it from my mother. But does that mean my mother is here? Is she a Tech? A captive of the AI? Or is she like Bear and gone back into the ground?

For a moment, longing sweeps into me. I want to reach out and touch her hair, to stroke the dark brown strands. She wears my mother's face and my mother's hair wound up in the back. It lays perfectly flat and smooth. Her face is oval with a chin that tapers to almost a point. The high cheekbones and hollows below them and the sharp jawline make her seem angular, but my fingertips tingle. Her skin will be soft—my mother's skin was soft. Her long lashes sweep down as she blinks, and her eyes…they are wrong. I know this. The eyes glow blue and so very bright. Not even Skye has eyes that color. That is how I know this really is the AI. No one's eyes look like that.

I swallow and push my shoulders back. "I'm helping Raj. I'm supposed to find the Glitches but I can't do that without him." I keep my voice firm and even. She tips her head to the side as though studying me. But this is a projection. She is a machine. And I know the AI is trying to manipulate me just as she does the Techs.

"Of course you can."

"No, I can't. One Glitch leads to another—I need this Glitch to find the others." This is a gamble. I do not know the AI sent me to look for Glitches, but the AI seems to have reason to want me around. And why else would the AI send the Techs after Raj but not after me? I very much fear the AI is the one who gave me a purpose.

Glancing at the screen, I can't see Raj—just a swarm of Techs.

Forcing myself to look away from that image, I look at Conie. "If he becomes nonfunctional, the task of finding Glitches fails. Is that what you want?"

I know if I try to override the AI controls over the Techs, Conie will undo my work. But I'm getting frustrated. I bunch my fists at my side. Nothing I try is working. I glance at the screen. When I look back, Conie is gone. Will it work now?

Hands flying, I call up the schematic. It changes—and it's not my doing.

Conie's voice echoes in the virtual room. "You have one cycle to leave with the Glitch."

Glancing at the screen, the one projecting Raj, I can see the Techs freeze and then slowly back away. Raj sits up, red dripping from his nose and from gashes on his face. He is holding one arm close.

I have no idea how long one cycle is, and I don't have time to worry about it. I unhook the connect and step away from the building. I'm back in the Norm. Turning, I hurry to Raj.

The Techs stroll away. They don't even glance at me or Raj. Kneeling down beside him, I put an arm around him and urge him to stand. “Get up. The AI gave us one cycle to leave and I don’t think that’s a long time.”

He staggers to his feet and leans heavily on me. I don’t mind. It’s easier than I expected to shoulder his weight. “Which way is out?”

Shaking his head, he tries to turn and pulls against me. “Can’t. So close.”

“You were so close to permanent nonfunctionality. We go. Now. This isn’t open for argument.”

“Lib?” His voice is pleading, and so is the look he gives me. But one eye is swelling shut and turning purple. His cloth is torn and one arm hangs at his side as if it hurts to move it.

“You’re hurt, and we’re on a clock to go. You want to see me end up nonfunctional, too?” It is an empty threat. I know this, but Raj doesn’t. The AI wants me functional. Conie wants me to find the Glitches. I don’t know why, but I don’t think it’s for anything good. I’ll worry about that later. Right now, I need to get Raj—and myself—out of here and back to the tunnels.

Raj’s mouth pulls down and his eyebrows flatten, but the Techs start to turn back to face us. His resistance drains out like water onto the sand. “Okay, but we will come back,” he tells me fiercely.

I nod. “We will. But we need a better plan.” Much better, I think.

Chapter Fifteen

The desert heat hits like that blast I saw from the drone. It is so intense I stumble and sink to the ground with Raj. After the Norm, the Outside seems stark and brown. The wall slides closed behind us. My side aches from running and my shoulders burn from half carrying Raj outside. He slumps on the ground, the cut on his face bleeding sluggishly now. Dried blood cakes his nose. The Norm was beautiful—so cool—but I don't want to think about it. I don't want to think about the AI. I just have to get Raj and me away from here.

For a moment, I can't move. My arms and legs have no strength. But we can't stay. We lost the water skins. I still have my pouch, and the fruit from the Norm, but I want to keep that in case we are out here for more than a day. For now, we need to get out of the sun.

I tug at Raj and tell him that.

He nods and struggles to his feet. Pulling his arm over my shoulder I take some of his weight on me. At least he's light enough I can manage with him.

I glance back behind us, and the wall of the Norm is smooth again—seamless. Will the AI send drones after us? It's possible. With that in mind, I stagger with Raj to the platform. It at least gives us some shade. Leaving Raj leaning against the platform, I make a connect. This time I know what I'm looking for—drones. It's easy to find the line of light that leads to them. Even easier to pluck the light that sends them all for maintenance and recharging. I slip out of the disconnect as fast as I can. I don't want the AI to notice me. Conie probably will—eventually. But I want to be far from here by then.

I glance back at the Norm, and a twinge of regret pinches in my chest.

I am leaving again.

It is my choice this time. Was it mine before? Is the purpose I thought I had—to find the Glitches—really the AI's purpose for me? I no longer know what I am. All I can hang onto is that I am Lib—for now, that has to be enough. I'll deal with the questions later.

Turning away from the Norm, I glance at Raj. He wipes the red from his face with his sleeve. "You're just smearing it," I tell him.

He makes a face. "We should wait here until the sun's lower."

I look at the sky. I can see the sun is halfway up and halfway down. I look at Raj again. "I sent the drones to maintenance. That won't keep them away forever, and I don't trust the AI not to come after us again."

After you. That's what I think. For some reason, the AI has a purpose for me. That's even more frightening than the AI sending Techs and drones after me.

I slap Raj's shoulder and drag his arm over me again. "We'll take it slowly."

The wind picks up, throwing sand into my face. I put my head down and stare at the tips of my weathered boots. Sweat drips down my back and beads on my forehead, trickling into my eyes. The stinging of it at least distracts from the bite of the sand.

Raj keeps his head down, too, and staggers along next to me. We reach the rocks and I find a small patch under the overhang of a cliff. I let go of Raj and lean against the smooth, cool side of the rock.

Raj drops to his knees next to me. "Lib, thank you. I don't know how you got us out."

He tries to smile but ends up wincing. I straighten and run my hands down his arms. When I touch his side, he flinches away. "You may have something broken."

He looks up and lifts a hand but lets it fall back to the dirt. "Broken is better than nonfunctional."

"Better would be if we had managed to get to the AI and shut it down. Conie's going to make it even harder to get close to her."

He stares at me, eyes narrowed. "Conie?"

“Uh…long story. Do you think any of the plants around here have water?”

He nods. “The ones with spikes on them. You need a knife to cut them open and get to the liquid inside.”

I scoot deeper into the shade. The sun is moving and this spot will soon be in sunlight again. I think about Wolf’s knife—the sharp metal he gave to Bear. It makes me more determined to get back to the tunnels. I put a hand on my pouch. The fruit is still there, but should we eat it? Will we need it later?

Raj’s hand falls on my shoulder. “I shouldn’t have tried this. I owe you.”

I shake my head, but I am too tired to argue. And he is right. We shouldn’t have tried this. But now I have a few more memories and a lot more questions. For now, we need to rest. Raj slumps against the cliff. We will wait until the shade is gone and then start walking.

I close my eyes for a moment. When I open them, the shade is gone and it is time to move. I struggle to my feet and nudge Raj’s shoulder with a hand.

Then I hear the soft hum.

My heartbeat thuds harder. It could be a drone. But it seems to echo from the rocks ahead of us. “Raj, do you hear it?”

Raj mutters but doesn’t wake.

I climb up on the rock that was shading us and put one hand over my eyes to try and see better. A column of dust rises up in the distance. The hum is coming closer. Squinting, I can just make out what looks like an AT, the cage glinting a little in the sunlight.

I scramble back to Raj and lean down to shake his shoulder. "Raj, wake up. Someone's coming."

I help Raj to his feet. I don't know why a single AT is out. Maybe it's a scavenge. I just don't want to miss whoever it is seeing us. Raj and I stagger back up onto the rock. The AT is closer this time.

I let go of Raj, and I wave my hands over my head. Raj gives a shout and waves with one arm. The AT shifts course slightly and heads toward us. I scramble down from the rocks, my palms scraping on a rough edge, and Raj follows me. Relief mixes with anxiety. Will they stop? What will Wolf think of us when we return? Will we be in more trouble?

Do they have water?

The AT hums to a stop, and Bird pulls down a cloth she has wrapped around her mouth and head. This AT is bigger than the others, with what look like four seats in it, though it is skeletal and the metal looks streaked with red and half rusted.

"Bird?" My voice is so dry it cracks. I head over to her and put a hand on the AT, slumping against it. "What are you doing here?"

She glances from me to Raj and back, and then says, "I was looking for you."

"Wolf let you? I didn't think anyone would come after us."

"Well, he was…worried."

She looks away when she says this. A flush of heat washes through me, but it cools at once. There's something here Bird is not saying.

"How did you know where to look?"

Bird's mouth hangs open. Her eyes widen. She glances again at Raj and pulls at one of the loose ribbons in her hair. Letting go of the ribbon, she waves her hand wildly, and then says, "We have to get Raj to the clan. He looks like he needs Croc."

That isn't an answer, but she is right. Bird swings off the AT and comes over to help Raj into the back seat. Bird gives a sniff and says, "You stink. That's not going to help."

With a groan, I settle next to Bird. "Help with what?"

Bird smiles, tugs the cloth back over her face and gets on the AT. She turns it on, and after that there's no asking questions or answering them. She doesn't give me a headset and the wind whips away my words. And I keep thinking one thing.

What aren't you telling us, Bird?

*   *   *

Riding gives time for my muscles to tighten up. I seem to be sore everywhere. Raj must be even worse off. When the AT hits a bump, Raj bites off a groan. And Bird is right—Raj stinks of sweat and blood now.

Just like with the other ATs, we leave this one covered a long walk from the tunnels. Leaving the AT is hard. I want to take it all the way back. But with Bird on one side of Raj and me on the other, we get him and ourselves back. Inside, we take Raj to Croc.

Bird pushes at me to leave. "Go. Clean up."

I glance down. My tunic is dusty. So are my boots and pants. More dust and sand cakes my skin. With a tired nod, I leave Raj to Croc and Bird.

Just as I step into the main room, a large hand reaches out and grabs me by the upper arm. I am pulled around to face Wolf.

My breath catches on a sharp gasp. His dark eyes bore down into mine. I swallow.

"What were you thinking?" he demands. He puts his other hand on my other arm and pulls me closer to him. It's impossible to be aware of anything other than his muscles, his size, and the snapping brightness in his eyes.

My mind, however, seems to have gone nonfunctional, leaving just my body moving. My heart is beating faster, but I like the feel of Wolf's hands on me. It's as if I'm in a connect, but a good one—a grounding one. I know who I am with Wolf.

I also know if I tell Wolf the truth, he won't understand. I cannot tell any of the Rogues about my encounter with the AI. If they thought I was bad luck before, they will think I am even worse if they hear my purpose might well be the AI's purpose, too.

So I lie.

"Raj and I wanted to try a bigger connect—and a hack. We thought we could get not just access to the Norm, but a larger supply of water. And…and food." I remember the fruit in my pouch. I pull out one now and hold it up between us, offering it to Wolf.

He leans back, stares at it, and then pulls me closer so my hands and the fruit are caught between our bodies. "If Bird hadn't had her vision—" He breaks off.

"Vision? What do you mean? We…we just wanted to be…be useful."

His eyes narrow. "Two Glitches on their own. How long would you last out there? That's not being useful to throw your life away. That's being a stupid, broken Glitch!"

The words sting. I don't know what to say to him.

He lets out a shuddering breath, and I catch a glimpse of worry in his eyes.

I bite my lower lip and try to push the fruit up higher so he will see it. "We got food—fruit."

He drops his hands from me and says, "I want a promise you'll never try a connect again with just you and another Glitch."

His voice holds so much intensity. But I cannot make that promise. I've already told Raj we will go back to the Norm, and we can't do that with Rogues. With Wolf looking at me now, his eyes so dark and hopeful, I want to tell him what he wants to hear. Should I lie again? And keep it up—over and over?

I shake my head. "I need to be useful. You said I'm a Glitch. That means I need to make connects. You won't survive out here. Glitches won't survive. We all do what we have to."

He shakes his head, but the corner of his mouth lifts into the tiniest of smiles. "Yeah. Then you're going to have to learn to survive in the Outside."

I blink at him and tighten my hand around the fruit. I wasn't expecting this.

He steps back and folds his arms across his broad chest. "And I'm going to teach you."

I swallow hard. Somehow, Wolf doesn't make that sound like it is going to be fun—or easy.

Chapter Sixteen

Wolf doesn't make it easy on Raj, either.

Raj is still meant to rest due to Croc's orders. But Raj and Wolf share yells that are so loud, they echo down the tunnels. Wolf's deep growl says something about Raj leaving, and almost everyone hears Raj say, "You don't own me and half the time you don't even want the Glitches here."

It gets quiet after that. I glance at Skye, but she presses her lips tightly and will not say anything.

I head over to see Raj. Wolf is gone. Raj will be able to self-repair, but his bruises look terrible in shades of black and purple with edges of yellow that don't blend with his smooth skin tone. The other Glitches, Chandra and Marq, come by and ask to hear everything about the Norm. I am more than happy to slip away and let Raj tell them. Because I have to train.

Training for me begins with two young Rogues—both girls with dark hair and eyes—who look at me like I must be stupid to be my age and need to be taught things.

Wolf meets me and the two young Rogues in the main room. He glances at the young ones, nods to me, and heads down one of the tunnels that lead to an exit. Wolf wears the dark pants and same black boots as always, but his shirt is different. It is cloth and hugs his wide shoulders and chest, showing off his muscles. He looks like he did in my dream last night.

The dream had Wolf and Raj in it, and an animal that howls its last breath into the night. I don't understand it but am grateful it was not the image of blackness that swallows up everyone.

I let the two young Rogues follow Wolf and I follow them. When I climb up the rope and step into the Outside, the heat makes me want to turn around and go back. But Wolf is already walking ahead of us, followed by the two young Rogues.

Just like always, no one speaks. I don't mind. No one—except the other Glitches—asks about the Norm, and I don't want to talk about it. I worry now that the Rogues will find out somehow that the AI gave me a purpose—to find the Glitches. I worry even more that once I do, it is not going to be for a good reason. But who can I tell?

The AI seems to be everyone's enemy—except Conie did not send Techs after me. What does that mean?

Keeping my eyes on the ground, I follow the Rogues. Wolf stops and so do the young ones. I almost bump into them. Wolf shakes his head and says, "You need to walk softly. Quietly. Walk toe first." He hesitates then says, "We're not going far, so practice."

The two young Rogues swap smiles and one snorts out a breath. I frown at them. I can do what Wolf asks. I nod to show I'm listening.

Wolf starts walking.

We trail after him, single file. Walking toe first makes my steps quiet, but soon my calves and feet ache. Sweat makes my tunic stick to my back. The sun beats down hot and hard. I have to squint to see. I realize no one has any pouch. No one has any water skin.

Looking up, I call out, "Wolf, did you forget the water?"

The two young Rogues snort again, and Wolf glances back. "We'll find what we need."

That doesn't sound encouraging. What if I find nothing?

We reach the boulders and I know what to expect now. Wolf pulls the cloth off one boulder, turning it from a huge rock into a cage vehicle—an AT like the one Bird rode to find me and Raj. Wolf rolls up the cloth rock and stuffs it into a bag strapped to the back of the vehicle. I won't have to hold on to Wolf like I'd had to do with Raj, and disappointment creeps into me. I shake my head. I don't need this attraction to Wolf and neither does he.

Wolf hands out headsets that we all put on. Once we're all in our seats, Wolf starts the AT and heads off, making his own road it seems. His voice sounds metallic over the headsets. "The wastelands are just what they sound like. There is little but waste in them, and they don't forgive you for wasting anything either. The Norm uses up just about everything—water, plants, animals for food. But the AI's drones miss things. They see nothing but rock and sand."

"And they look for us." This comes from one of the young ones.

I try to ignore them, but Wolf nods and says, "That's right, Mouse. Sometimes, they're so busy looking for us—or for water—they miss the animals that know how to hide. They fly over the plants that hoard water like we do. Everything you need is here—if you know how to find it."

"That is a very large if," I mutter.

The headset picks it up, but Wolf just grins at me. It's the first time I have seen a grin on him. He is enjoying this. I stiffen my back and stare straight ahead. I am not going to keep asking stupid questions.

Wolf stops the AT near yet another outcropping of rocks. This one seems to be some distance from the Norm. I cannot see its walls. He pulls the rock-colored cloth from the bag and covers the AT. Glancing at the Rogues, and then at me, he says, "A drone looks for what doesn't belong. We need the AT to look like a rock. We need to look like we belong, too."

“What about the tracks?” I gesture back to the lines left in the dust by the AT.

Wolf straightens. “Watch.”

As I do, the wind comes up. It slips across the line left by the AT. In a short time, there are no more tracks. Frowning, I glance at Wolf. “If the wind does that, why not leave the ATs closer to the tunnels? Why walk so much.”

One of the Rogues—Mouse again, I think—says, “The drones don’t just look for tracks—they’ll scan for power sources, too. If they get a hit off an AT, we don’t want it near us. It has to look abandoned.”

Wolf nods and puts a hand on Mouse’s head. “When are drones out?”

“Night,” I answer.

Both young Rogues give me pitying glances, and the other one says, “Mostly night. But the AI isn’t stupid. If drones aren’t finding us or Glitches at night, it’ll start sending out drones in the day. We have to keep changing it. Keep moving. Law is we protect the clan.”

With a sharp nod, Wolf smiles. “That’s right, Mole.” Wolf checks that the cloth is tied down over the AT so it can’t blow away. He straightens, glances around, and checks the sky before motioning for us to follow. He slips down a rocky slope, half sliding. Mouse and Mole follow him as if it is easy. I scrape my hands and hear cloth tear, but I get my boot on the ground. Wolf crouches low. Mouse and Mole copy him. I do, too, but I crane to see why we are doing this.

Grabbing the hem of my tunic, Wolf tugs me even lower and over next to him so we are shielded by low rocks and spindly bushes. He points ahead with his other hand and whispers, "See it?"

His breath tickles my ear. It's warm and sweet. I want to shift away, but I can't. Next to me, Mouse and Mole each nod. I squint into the bright day.

At first, I see sand, rocks, more bushes as brown as the ground. Irritation claws at me, mixing with disappointment. I am failing, and it is too early to fail. But a flicker of movement—a quick shift in the tans and browns—catches my eye. I stare at that one spot. My eyes start to water. I can barely breathe. It moves again—a small, skinny animal of some kind with a tail and four legs and its belly on the ground.

"I see it," I whisper. A touch of pride flickers through me.

Wolf keeps his voice low and soft. "That's just a small thing. A lizard. But the lizard is clever. He comes out in morning to drink dew from the plants and finds shade during the day. Then he finds bugs to eat at night."

Mouse nods and says, “Lizard is determined. My brother’s named Lizard.”

Her voice startles the lizard into running away and disappearing into a hole. Mole slaps Mouse’s arm. Wolf stands and puts his hands on his hips. “Lizard is smarter than you, Mouse. Lizard knows to lose his tail to keep his life. He changes color to blend in with the world.” Turning, he holds out a hand. “Look not just with your eyes. Be like the lizard. Smell the world. Taste the wind. Listen for what moves.”

Slowly, I stand. I brush at the dust and try to do as Wolf asks. But how do you taste wind? I only taste dust. How do you smell things? I look around us until my eyes sting. My throat is dry. I kick at a rock with my boot. “I don’t see anything.”

“I see a tree?” Mole says. Mouse nods and points.

I look and behind the shrubs there is a tree, its bark so pale that it seems dead. It has twined itself between the rocks until it looks more like lines on the rock than a plant. I remember the fruit trees in the Norm. They were tall and straight and dark green. Nothing like this. Shaking my head, I say, “It’s dead.”

“No, it’s not.” Mouse gives me another of her pitying looks. It takes everything in me not to reach over and pull at her dark hair.

“It’s a great trick,” Mole says. “Look dead and no one looks at you twice.”

Wolf shakes his head. "Not everything. We scavenge—others do, too. Some animals are happy to clean up the dead."

Crossing my arms, I glance at the tree again. "If it's alive, it needs water." I know this much is fact. The trees and grass in the Norm are alive because the AI takes the water. That is why it is so green in the Norm. But why does the AI need all the water?

A small smile tugs on Wolf's mouth. My skin warms for I put it there. "Now you are looking. Trees will lead you to water. So will the lizard and other animals if you go follow them. We have to be like this tree. We store as much as we can, use as little as we need, and wait for the next rain."

"Or the next hack."

Now Mouse and Mole stare at me, eyes narrowed—as if they are thinking I am not so stupid.

I close my eyes and lift my head to pull in a breath. I can smell the tree better than I can see it. It has a dry, sharp scent. What else can I smell? With my eyes closed, I hear a distant cry—a bird maybe. I open my eyes and look around. I still see so very little. Has the AI taken everything? Why does it need so much?

Wolf leads us from the lizard to another area and points out more survivors. He uses his knife to cut open a cactus for water. It tastes funny and it's warm. But it wets my lips. Now I want a knife like Wolf's. I see that Mouse and Mole each have their own knives, and they dig out white flesh from inside the cactus and eat it. Wolf takes us to a rabbit den. We wait for a long time but nothing comes out of the small hole. An animal that looks like a wolf but smaller, pads over to the rabbit hole and looks in. Wolf calls it a coyote.

When the coyote leaves, we follow its tracks. Mouse tells me that a coyote is clever enough to live off almost anything—plants or animals. "Rogues are like coyotes."

Wolf stops us near more rocky hills but still a distance from the AT. I wait, sweat on my forehead and upper lip, looking around, trying to smell and hear and figure out what Wolf sees. He stares at the rocks. Mouse and Mole edge closer to each other. The back of my neck tingles and I look up a little.

An animal that is like the wolf, but not at all like it, sits up on the rocks. It has a black face and a tan body and a long tail that flicks with what looks like irritation to me. It gets up and slinks away. Mouse lets out a breath and mutters, "Mountain cat. Good eating if they don't eat you first."

Wolf glances at Mouse. "What's the law?"

She frowns and shuffles a foot into the dirt. "Kill only when the clan must eat and waste nothing."

He gives a small nod. I think again about all the fruit in the Norm. There was more than enough to feed everyone I saw in the

Norm—and have some left. It suddenly seems so unfair that the Techs have so much and the Rogues so little.

And where do the Glitches fit into this?

They were Techs, but now they're living more like Rogues. Do they have to learn the Rogues' law? Do they follow it?

The sun is starting down. Wolf keeps us out to see the animals start to come out from hiding from the sun. We see both a mouse and a mole, and they are nothing like the two Rogue girls with us, but the girls grin to have seen the animals they were named for. Wolf tells stories in that deep voice of his, how the mole can find its way in any tunnel and how the mouse has to be smart enough to avoid the great birds that hunt at night.

My stomach grumbles a little. We have had nothing to eat. Wolf tells us to find plants for our meal. Mouse and Mole run off to do just that. I can only think of the cactus, but there are none here. Sitting down, I wonder if I could go back and catch that poor, little lizard. My stomach tightens, but I would eat it if I had nothing else. And if I could catch it.

"Why don't we hunt something?" I ask, looking up at Wolf.

He sits down next to me. "You want to hunt with your bare hands? Besides, we have meat back at the clan. This is about what to do if you're out here with nothing."

I nod and glance around. I want the fruit that is back in my pouch at the tunnels.

I hear a tearing and glance over to see Wolf pulling up a small clump of grass. He brushes off the roots and pulls one off. “Try this. Learn what is good by smell and rub it on your skin. If it burns, doesn’t smell sweet or smells like a drone, it’s bad.”

After staring at the root, I take it. Wolf pops a root into his mouth. I do the same. It is sweet. I am ready to eat more, but Wolf only gives me one root at a time. “Chew slow. Waste nothing.”

We have eaten all the grass roots by the time Mouse and Mole get back. They have a green pod that Wolf throws toward the rabbit hole, saying, “Not ripe.” He approves of the flowers they pick—they are bright orange and taste bitter, but I like them.

In the distance, I hear a soft hum. Everyone holds very still. The hum goes away, and Wolf stands. He says nothing, just starts to walk. Going back to the ATs, I hope. I am certain the hum came from a drone. We get back to the AT without hearing another drone. The night seems far more alive than the day. I hear distant howls and the sound of bird wings flapping. The wind brings the smell of something sweet nearby.

How long will it take me to learn the names of everything?

Near the AT, I stop and stare out over the land. It looks different with the stars to light it—softer and more alive. I see the flash of an animal's eyes as it watches us. I can see why the Rogues would rather come out at night—so would most things. But drones are out, too. I see another distant flash, this one in the sky. A light blinks—steady on and off. That is a drone from the AI scanning the hills where we were today.

Wolf starts the AT. This time we don't wear headsets, and no one seems to want to talk. I think maybe Mouse and Mole are as tired as I am. The trip back is bumpy. Wind brushes sand into my face. This time I try to taste it to see what it will tell me, but it only tells me I am thirsty. The AT stops and I blink. Are we back? But no—we have to walk yet. Wolf covers up the AT, and then we walk back to the tunnels. I am too tired to practice being silent, and I hope Wolf is too tired to notice. But he glances back at me now and I am certain he is frowning, even though I can't see his expression.

I make a face at him and hear a muffled giggle from Mouse. She makes a face back, so I make one at her again. That gets us both another glance from Wolf.

Walking, staying a couple of steps behind the others, I watch Wolf's back. His stride is long, but not so long that Mouse, Mole and I can't keep up. He is making sure of that. He's so big. How can he be so quiet? Sometimes—like now—he seems so much older than me. But he's not. It is only when he gives that rare grin that he looks young.

But I can see why the Rogues follow him. I feel that pull, that desire to please, to get one of those smiles of his.

Heading down the tunnels, Mouse and Mole run ahead of us. I hear the patter of their boots on the stone of the tunnel. Wolf stays with me.

When we walk into the main room, it seems as if the Rogues all glance at me. Is that suspicion in their eyes? Did they hear about me and the AI? Do they know my purpose is to find the Glitches for the AI?

I shiver and wrap my arms around myself.

Wolf's large hand rests against the small of my back. Startled, I look up and see him staring back at the Rogues. He seems to be saying something. The others look away.

I don't know what this means, but the warmth of Wolf's hand spreads through me.

But my purpose is to find the Glitches. That thought pushes at me, and I push back.

This is helping me fulfill my purpose. The need to do what the AI wants me to do fades. For now, I have it under control. How long will that last?

Chapter Seventeen

Wolf shakes his head and says, "Move faster."

I'm panting and sweat trails down my back beneath the thin shirt I borrowed from Bird. She tossed it at me when she heard Wolf was training me. That was now almost one full moon ago.

Skye stands on a rock nearby and yells, "You can do it, Lib!"

It is early morning—so very early the sun is not even visible. We stand on top of a hill. A few rocks surround a smooth, sandy area. That is where Wolf and I stand. I am supposed to learn to fight.

Raj sits beside Skye, not far from us. He is repaired, but he and Wolf seem to avoid each other. However, Raj watches now as Wolf tries to teach me to defend myself.

I massage my left shoulder. Wolf punched me there. I can be strong when I am threatened or when I must do something seemingly impossible. But this gift does not come alive when I am training.

Because it isn't real.

Well, a connect isn't real, either. But it is far more dangerous. A connect is live currents that can kill. Wolf could, too, but the blow to my shoulder only stings. It has half the force of what it could have. Maybe less.

Ignoring the way Bird's shirt sticks close, I lift my hands again. Bird is much smaller. Her shirt stops just above my waist, showing my navel and the bones of my hips where my pants hang loosely. It is comfortable to have air on my belly, but I am used to my tunic.

Wolf comes at me again, moving fast. Power is speed, he keeps telling me, and I am beginning to understand. But the reverse is not true. But I am fast.

Speed is my greatest ally. I wait until Wolf is practically on top of me, and then I duck and slide my foot at the same time. I throw a kick that catches his hip. It isn't enough to do much of anything.

Wolf steps back and shakes his head. But his mouth curves up. "Better. But we have to do strength building. I barely even felt that."

"Love tap!" Skye shouts out.

I have no idea where she learned that term. I wave her off and lean over to catch my breath. When I look over at Skye, I see Raj frowning. He folds his arms across his chest.

In the next instant, Wolf's leg hits my knee. With one wide sweep, he knocks me on my butt. I hit and let out a gust of air.

Standing over me, he says, "Don't get distracted." He holds out a hand. I take it and he pulls me back to my feet.

"I don't really know why this is important. Am I supposed to fight animals or something?" I wet my lips and think of the Techs crowding Raj. Would this have helped me then? But there were so many. I couldn't have fought them all.

Wolf leans down and picks up a skin of water. He unstops the top and hands me the skin. I sip at it. Waste nothing—use only what you need. Wolf is also teaching me law. "Do you expect me to fight?" I let the words trail off. Do I have to fight Rogues? Glitches? Uneasy now, I shift on my feet.

He gives me a sharp look and then takes a breath. Does he still think I know so little? I am learning, and while I still dream, they do not leave me shaking. I also control my urge now to find the Glitches.

This will help my purpose.

That thought is one I cling to. But will it work forever?

Wolf frowns and says, "Rogues don't fight within the clan."

"Meaning clans sometimes fight other clans?" I ask.

He shakes his head. "Life is hard enough. But…not all Glitches come out like you or Skye." He glances at Raj. "Or even like Raj."

Raj gives a loud snort, and Skye cries out, "Hey!"

Wolf ignores her. "Glitches have tried to hurt people. Some have even been spies sent by the AI. It was obvious becausc they asked too many questions. It's why Rogues don't trust them."

My throat tightens. I swallow but it doesn't go down, so I bite my lower lip. Am I a spy? But my purpose is to find Glitches, not Rogues. And then I glance at Wolf. "Them." I mutter the word. Wolf said them, not you.

But if I am not a Glitch, what am I?

I open my mouth to ask more questions—just what Wolf said a spy Glitch would do. I snap my mouth shut and turn away.

Bobcat appears behind Skye and Raj. She gives me a sideways look and turns her full attention to Wolf. "You're needed."

Wolf nods. He starts to follow Bobcat and then turns to me. "Strength." He grabs my arm and squeezes the muscle. I flinch. "More strength."

He follows Bobcat, heading for the tunnels. I walk over to Skye and Raj. She bounds up to her feet. "You're doing great."

"I wish. But I'm glad you think so."

We head back to the tunnels. Raj seems too quiet.

Once inside the cool darkness, I let out a breath. It is almost chilly since I am still sweating. I need a cloth so I can wipe down.

Skye skips ahead of Raj and me saying, "I'm going to see if I can scrounge up something to eat." She wrinkles her nose. "And sage to rub into your skin. You smell."

Before I can swat at her, she runs off. I glance at Raj to ask if he is going to eat, too. The look in his eyes—it seems like pain—stops me.

"What are you trying to do—give up being a Glitch and become a Rogue?"

I blink and step back as if his words were punches. "I am trying to learn. And what's so wrong with fitting in?"

He gives a frustrated growl and steps closer. He leans down. I see spots of gold in his otherwise dark eyes. "You're not like them… and you're not like us, are you?"

My face goes cold.

Not like us

Not a Glitch.

It hurts to hear him say this. Fear shivers through me. What if others think this? What if others find out I spoke to the AI—that Conie has a purpose for me. That I am a tool of the AI.

Wolf just said Rogues don't trust Glitches because of that. Will Wolf turn away from me? Will all the Glitches? Or will it be worse? Will the Rogues turn away from all Glitches?

I know Raj, Skye, Chandra and Marq can't survive without the Rogues. Even I am still learning how to get by in the Outside. Without the Rogues, how long would any of us last in the Outside?

Is this why the AI wants me to find the Glitches—to bring them back to the Norm? But if that was true, why wasn't Raj welcomed back?

I shake my head. I want to argue, but I can't force the words out. My chest hurts and my stomach cramps.

"I don't know why, Lib." Raj puts his hands on my shoulders. "You're special. You're better."

My eyebrows shoot up. "What? Better? Since waking up in the desert, I've thought of myself as many things, but not…Raj, you're wrong."

Raj's hands tighten and his fingers dig into my skin. "You are. You got us into the Norm and got us out. You're going to do amazing things." He glances down the tunnels and then looks back at me. "Don't let all of this make you lose sight of your real skills."

"The connect," I mutter. I pull away. I don't want to connect to the AI—not even to a subroutine. I'm having enough trouble without any more contact with Conie.

But Raj smiles at me. “Tomorrow, you’re with me. I’m taking you out and we’ll practice some hacking.”

Chapter Eighteen

The next day I go out with Raj, but we don't go out alone. Bobcat and several other Rogues go with us. I don't know their names and no one bothered to tell them to me. Wolf isn't with us. When I ask Bobcat why, she says, "He can't be expected to hold your hand every day."

My face heats. "Did I ask for that?"

I turn away and head over to Raj's AT. His bruises yellow his skin and his moves are stiff, but he smiles at me. "I'll hold your hand."

My face warms again. I shake my head and swing a leg over the AT. We ride the small ones, and I wrap my arms around Raj. He flinches and gives a groan. I loosen my grip. "Still hurts?"

"Only when I laugh," he mutters.

Bobcat gets on her AT with another Rogue. She leads the way. We follow her for several miles, winding through dusty canyons until the cliffs open up into an almost grassy area. The grass is thin and grows in clumps, but it looks like the grass Wolf showed me how to eat.

Bobcat slows and comes to a stop. I glance around, remembering what Wolf said. I close my eyes and listen and smell. I can smell faint traces of oil, and I hear wind whistling through metal. Opening my eyes, I see a platform buried by sand.

I get off the AT and head over to the platform. It's in worse shape than any I have seen. But it must be connected still. My hands are clammy, my nerves eating at me. I don't want to explain why I don't want to connect.

Raj goes down on his knees and brushes away the sand. He exposes a railing. The platform fell on its side—half is buried, but the railing is near the top. He grins. "The more obscure, the less likely the AI will be monitoring this platform. We still have to be careful. The sentinels still patrol every connect."

I nod but don't step any closer to the platform. I don't want to go in. I never want to go in again. If I go in, will Conie let me out? Will Conie tell me things I don't want to hear? Will I be reminded of my purpose?

I rub the sweat from my palms on my pants. The back of my neck is tingling and I want to rub it, too, but that would make it obvious how nervous I am.

Raj waves me forward, but I hesitate.

My hands are shaking. My heart pounds and my breath is fast and uneven. I am scared of going in there. I can still remember the AI and… and I don't know why she helped me or why she had my mother's face. For all I know, she has my mother somewhere in the Norm. Maybe she holds my mother hostage to use to force me to do what Conie wants. These are things I'm not ready to deal with yet, but I don't have a choice. I can't tell Raj about any of this—certainly not with Bobcat and the other Rogues watching us and watching the skies.

"Hurry," Raj says. A flicker of irritation grates his voice. "You want to wait here until a drone flies by?"

I have no way out. I force myself to walk three steps forward, my heart pounding so loudly I am certain everyone can hear it. I stand beside Raj. The wind hums through the rusted metal. Maybe it will be fine. Maybe there is no power to this platform anymore. Maybe it is nonfunctional and nothing will happen when I try a connect.

Maybe I am dreaming.

Raj gives a tight nod. "Connect. I'll let you know what we're looking for once we're inside."

Before I can agree or disagree, he places his hand on the railing. His eyes glaze over, unfocused and distant until it seems as if his body is an empty shell. I hadn't thought about how a connect must look to others, but now I glance at the Rogues. They look away and shift uneasily. It must seem to them that Raj isn't really out here anymore. Which is true. His mind is tucked inside a vast computer right now, floating in an endless flow of data.

I can't leave him there on his own. He might encounter sentinels. Or Conie.

With a steadying breath, I force myself to reach out for the railing. The familiar prick of thousands of tiny pins stings my palm and I blink.

Connection: Secure.

I'm standing in a room, cool and blue and vast. Beside me on my left, rows and rows of what look like tall metal filing cabinets fade into the distance. They could just as easily be something else, but the words filing cabinets stick in my head. Raj is standing in front of me, and I am glad I connected next to him.

Relief prickles my skin at not seeing Conie. In the Norm, it almost seemed as if she knew where I was at all times and could sense every connect. But that must be only the Norm. It wasn't like that on other connects. The tightness in my chest eases.

Raj waves a hand. "We don't want to waste time. The longer we stay, the more likely it is the AI will notice us."

"We're looking for water, right?"

He nods. "We're always looking for water, but let's hold off on that today. Water is scarce enough that if we start a search, it'll activate sentinels."

Raj begins to walk between two rows of tall cabinets. They reach higher than I can see. I follow him, though I'm not sure I see the point. The world around us doesn't really change. It just shifts as we pass identical rows of filing cabinets. And why not just pull what we want? "What else would we be looking for?"

He glances back and grins. The quick flash of white teeth softens his features and brightens his dark eyes. It makes him look boyish and fun instead of bitter. I like him more when he's like this. "All kinds of things. Nutrients to add to the soil so maybe we could grow food again—like in the Norm. Access to seed storage. Even antidotes and medicines to help with poison or sickness."

"Don't we need to get that from the Norm?"

His grin fades. He hunches a shoulder and looks away. He is afraid of going back to the Norm—I know that now. "This is information storage—a place where everything is catalogued for easy reference. The physical goods will come from a storage facility in the Norm. When we find it, we're actually sending a request to transfer the materials to our location in the Outside."

"Don't you think it's strange to think of this world as not real?" I trail a hand over a cabinet. It is cool and hums a little. "In some ways, it's more real to me than anything. It's... familiar when the rest of the world is strange."

Raj isn't listening to any of this. His long stride carries him far ahead of me. I am not sure he would understand even if he heard me. Raising my voice, I ask, "Why don't we just search for the physical location of the storage so we can go get what we want when we want it?"

Raj glances at me, his eyebrows tugging down slightly, before he says, "Funny. Wolf asked the same thing."

"How is that funny? You're not smiling."

"It's an expression. And storage is within or under the Norm."

I nod. That says it all. Going inside the Norm is almost as hard as getting out again. Watching Raj, I frown now. Why is it that any mention I make of Wolf has Raj acting defensive?

"It's a good question," I tell him.

Raj continues walking. "I guess. It doesn't matter."

I shrug. "How do the materials get to the Outside? Drones? Something else? Doesn't the AI monitor that?" Isn't Conie watching everything?

"That's why we need to hack into a place where the AI isn't watching at that instant and get out again."

Now that he's said it, I feel stupid for even asking. This is the point of the hack. We use the connect for access and then use the hack to manipulate access. We are creating our own path to what we want.

As we walk, Raj talks about searches, how to concentrate on what you're looking for, and how to use multiple searches to make all of them seem ordinary. He glances back at me, his stares dark and calculating and adds, "Though, maybe you won't have to look."

I know he is thinking of how I brought the water to me, but I don't say anything. Raj turns and finds a ladder. We climb the massive towers of files, and Raj pulls out one drawer and then another. I feel as if I should look, too, so I just think of soil nutrients and seeds. A drawer opens for me. I glance at Raj. He is not looking. Like always I have lines of light spreading out in front of me. I pluck one. Half-invisible cubes, small enough to pocket, appear in the drawer. Raj still isn't looking. I pull out one and ask, "Is this what we want?"

Raj glances at me. His eyebrows flatten, but he nods. I don't heed Raj's caution not to take too much—my skin itches between my shoulder blades. We are being watched. I take three cubes and close the drawer.

As we climb back down and reach the floor, I notice a glittering ball. I move toward it, but Raj touches my arm. "That's just data. Mostly old data. The AI never deletes anything."

The ball pulls me. Data means information. Maybe it's data about me.

I almost don't want to touch it, but the colors are so bright—like one of the tiny flowers in the Outside. When I touch it, the access is instant. I absorb several terabytes before Raj pulls me away. "Are you okay? You went—I don't think you're supposed to go blank inside a connect."

Staring at him, I try to sort the data. I'm…stunned. "Raj, it was data. Did you know the Norm wasn't the only dome? There were dozens of them—cities all over the world. But the AI—Conie—shut them down and consolidated everyone here."

He frowns and tugs on my arm. "We have to go."

"No, the data. I want to know more. I don't know why she shut them down. There wasn't a Norm. It was domed cities, but now there's just the Norm. Conie's consolidating resources for some reason. She wanted everyone here. In one place. But those who wouldn't come into the domes got left out. And I didn't have time to find out the date on that."

Raj starts walking, pulling me with him. "If you keep accessing data, the sentinels are going to notice. And then the AI will. We have to go."

I turn back to catch a glimpse of the data orb, but it has already moved on. And now I have more questions. Why is there only one dome now? Why does the AI want all the resources of this world that Conie once called Earth?

Before I am ready, Raj breaks the connect. I am relieved, disappointed and angry with him. And I have much to think on. I am also itching for more data, and that could prove to be a dangerous thing for me and the Rogues.

Chapter Nineteen

Perfect neat rows lay at my feet, too many to count, but I know it is a perfectly square box.

A box of bodies.

It is worse because I am not horrified. Just detached. These are only bodies. And bodies are meant to be recycled. Whatever made the flesh and bones into something that could be called life is gone. There is nothing to do but accept such a fact. Nonfunctionality can only be reversed if the fault is one that can be corrected, such as a repair to the circuitry.

And if the desire to effect such a repair is in place.

I scan the lines of bodies. They could almost be sleeping, but they would breathe regularly in such a case. Some of the faces I recognize. I have seen them in the great room at the center of the tunnels where the clan gathers for meals and stories. Soon, names begin to flash across my mind—data unwinding.

Bobcat.

Lion.

Croc.

Bird.

I shudder now. Stop looking! Stop walking! I can't make my body listen.

When I see Skye, I choke. I want to scoop her up in my arms, to cradle her and smooth her hair. Those golden strands should be perfect. The desire to stop and touch and make this no longer real is overpowering, and yet I cannot stop walking. I want to fall to my knees and cry. But I walk on.

Raj is next. His black hair curls around his face and his skin seems paler but softer. His bitterness has melted away.

I tear my eyes away from his peaceful face, but I wish I hadn't. Because next is the last person I want to see.

Wolf.

His eyes are closed. His long, dark lashes lay still against his skin. Like Raj, he looks at peace. Is it easy to be nonfunctional? To be that way forever?

Falling to my knees, I reach out to touch Wolf's face and trail my fingertips across his cheek and the sharp line of his jaw.

"Wolf?" I ask, as though he is merely temporarily nonfunctional and might open his eyes.

But his skin is cold and stiff. What has happened?

Then I remember and I sit back on my heels. "It's all my fault."

Gasping for breath brings me alert. My vision blurs from the sting of tears, and I bite down on a wailing sob that lasts just long enough to create a short-lived echo.

This dream is worse than any other. I can still feel Wolf's cool skin beneath my fingertips. The ache vibrates in my heart at seeing them all dead—at seeing him dead.

I sit up because I can't stay lying down. Cold sweat chills me and my hands shake. I fold them together but can't stop the shaking.

I dart a glance around to make sure I haven't woken anyone. My dreams, though vivid and terrible, usually don't, but tonight I see glittering eyes staring back at me.

Bird is awake.

Her dark eyes seem huge. She seems to be assessing me and looking straight through to my darkest thoughts.

Her ribbons rustle and she asks, "Why do you always dream of death, Lib?"

Fear tightens like a band around my chest. I find myself shaking my head furiously. I stop that, gulp down a breath, and spit out, "Go back to sleep." I lie down, turn my back to her, and pretend to go back to sleep.

I won't sleep again tonight. My hands still shake and a weight settles on my chest as if some animal crouches there, making my breaths come in short, shallow gasps. I can't stop thinking about Bird's question.

Why do you always dream of death, Lib?

I don't know. But she's right.

I always do. Why?

*   *   *

Training with Wolf seems to give me tentative friendships with others. Bobcat no longer shoots me unfriendly looks, though we speak little. I am mostly certain that that is just how Bobcat is. Croc is friendly enough and will explain the properties of certain plants he uses. But I look for Wolf every morning and at meals.

And training gives us not just time together, but reasons to touch.

He comes at me with a punch, but I am faster. I wait until he is mere inches away and slide to the side, slipping away from his grasp like liquid.

I will never be as strong, but I am learning how to be quick as the wind that comes up in the evening.

I swivel around to come up behind him and wrap my arm around his neck, catching his throat in the corner of my elbow. The awkwardness of the height difference—he is much taller than me—makes him bend back slightly. That is enough for me to gain what leverage I need to twist and heave him over my hip. I let go and step away. With a grunt, he lands in the dirt.

Quickly, I move away before he has the chance to reach out for my leg and take me down with him. That is a mistake I no longer make.

He lets out a laugh—a low chuckle that warms my skin. The dust clears and I can't help but grin, too. Getting up, he pats my shoulder. "You learn quickly."

I'm grateful the training leaves me flushed. "I've had a good teacher."

He waves off my compliment. "You put in the work. I've never seen someone improve this fast."

I have to swallow hard. Is that really a good thing? Or is it like when Raj says I'm different. I want to fit in. I want the dreams to stop. I want to bask in Wolf's praise. Perhaps it is only my imagination, but I think his compliments come more frequently now.

But I worry.

What if he finds out the truth about me?

I already know Raj has not told the others about the data I discovered. I take his silence to mean I should not tell anyone either. The seed and nutrient cubes we took from the connect were left by a drone not far from the platform. We were able to pick them up without being seen. But I learned that day how dangerous connects really were. They weren't just dangerous inside the connect, but it was also difficult to go and take the materials brought to the Outside.

Wolf slaps my shoulder again, startling me. "I think we're done for the day," he says and tries to wipe away some of the dust from his face. It's not so easy because the dirt has mixed with his sweat to become like a fine coating of mud. I must look just as bad.

"Tired already?" I ask, teasing and light, hoping he takes it that way. I don't want to think about the AI—about Conie today. I just want to be with Wolf.

He shoots me a sideways glare, one eyebrow lifted, but it's not a real glare. "I'm saving you from eating dirt. Come, let's find something tastier."

We head back to the tunnels. I've learned to walk almost as silently as Wolf, and we walk single file. I know how to put my steps in his—fewer tracks to follow.

Down in the tunnels, Wolf touches my arm. This is not one of his friendly slaps. This touch has something else in it. Something seems to twist in my chest and I can't catch my breath. "I have to ask?" He lets the words trail off and does not ask.

I turn to look at him questioningly. "Wolf?"

He takes a deep breath before looking me in the eye and saying, “You’re ready now. I didn’t think it would happen so soon.”

My heart starts to pound. Is he going to ask me to leave? To tell me training is done and we will never meet like this in the mornings? My dream flashes into mind and my stomach gives a lurch. I put a hand over it. “What’s going to happen?”

He rakes a large hand through his thick dark hair. It is rare to see him nervous. “I mean… you can choose. To join the clan.”

I stare at him for a long time. He shifts on his feet, looks away, looks back and shifts again. My mouth seems dry but I finally process his words. “Become a Tracker?”

He gives a nod.

I can’t stop the grin that breaks across my face. Lunging at him, I throw my arms around his neck. His skin is hot against mine. “Of course. Yes. I want to! I choose.”

With a laugh, he twirls me around. I don’t want to ever let go.

* * *

After we eat, I tell the other Glitches. Well, I tell Raj and Skye, because Marq is getting the food and Chandra is turned away from us and seems completely uninterested.

“Seriously!” Skye’s blue eyes widen and seem as huge as the sky. I think of Bird staring at me, her eyes wide also.

Why do you always dream of death?

I push the thought away.

Dreams are only dreams. My purpose is to find Glitches and this will help. It’s all my fault.

The words all seem empty. I am no longer hungry and my smile fades, but I nod. “Wolf said I could choose.”

Skye laughs, but Raj is quiet and his eyes look troubled. I glance over at him. I see something unhappy and bitter in his eyes.

He stands and says, his tone sharp, “You don’t need to be a Tracker. This isn’t where we belong. Have you forgotten your promise?”

Skye glances at him. “What is your problem? And what promise?” She looks at me.

I put my stare on Raj. “I haven’t forgotten anything, and being a part of the clan doesn’t mean I will forget anything.”

Skye turns her back on Raj and takes my hand. “He’s just jealous because you were asked and he wasn’t.”

“That’s not it,” he snarls.

I believe him. Raj would never want to join the clan. He's angry I want to.

Skye tries to say something, but Raj slices the air with his hand. "If we fix the AI, we can go back. We can go back to our families."

Skye's smile drops away and she shifts and lets go of my hand. She looks troubled now.

A longing lifts inside me to return to a place I hardly remember. But I have seen the Norm. I know the beauty. Every connect leaves me wanting to go back. But now there is a war with an intense desire to stay. To become a part of this clan. "We didn't do such a good job last time," I shoot back at Raj.

He waves his arms wide. "We'll know better next time."

I shake my head. "So will the AI. It learns, too. And…and I like it here."

Raj barks out a laugh. "I know what you like. This is about Wolf. You like him. You really think the Rogues—that he—is ever going to really make you part of anything?"

My cheeks scald. I stand as well and face him, my fists bunched. I could put him on his ass, but I hold my anger back. "I can make a choice and keep my promise. But I'm not going to try to go back anytime soon."

“Of course not—Rogue.” Raj spits the word at me. Turning, he stalks off, muttering under his breath.

Her voice small, Skye asks, “What is Raj talking about? What promise did you make? Why does he think we could ever go back to the Norm?” She sounds bewildered.

I shake my head. I don’t know what to tell her. But someday I will have to keep my promise to Raj. I will have to go back. Closing my eyes, I want it to be a long, long time before that day comes.

But I fear I will never get that wish.

Chapter Twenty

Raj stops talking to me. Even Skye acts oddly now. She seems… stiff. It is like she must pick sides and didn't pick mine. Chandra and Marq are like they always are. They never talk to me anyway. Having the Glitches shut me out and not want to talk at meal times or even eat with me stings in a way I never thought it would. It hurts, but it doesn't change my decision.

I want this. I want to be a part of something.

Unfortunately, right now I'm not welcome by Glitches and I'm not really a Tracker.

Bobcat and Bird come to me and tell me the day of choice has come. This day is special.

They take me to a room in the tunnels that stinks. Water bubbles up from the ground, and steam gathers thick in the air. Bird says it is a hot spring. I stare at it and ask, "Why do we have to do connects for water if you have a spring right here? Just cool the water."

Bobcat laughs. "Try and drink that? Go ahead. It's full of things that could kill you. Croc's tried to filter them out, but it never works. It's only to wash, and only then on special days. Like today. Now get in."

I don’t like the idea of stepping into something that could kill me. But Bird and Bobcat strip off my boots and tunic and pants. I am not given a choice.

They tell me I have the springs all to myself. Ritual has made this day special.

Bird sits with me, cross-legged on the floor, not in the water, but close to it. She weaves strips of leather and shimmery beads into my hair. This, too, is needed on the day of choice.

“You did all of this, too?” I ask. She, too, has been quiet around me. Like Skye. I am not good friends with Bird, but I have never thought of her as hating me.

She nods and turns my head around again. “Long time ago, when I was saved.”

“Saved from what?” I ask.

She is quiet again. I glance back and see a flicker of emotion in her eyes. She pushes my head forward again. I don’t think she wants to tell me, but a moment later, her voice quiet, she says, “I am from the Sees Far clan. I was born to them and raised with their gifts. But my clan is gone back into the ground, devoured by the storm.” I can’t see her face but there is so much pain in her voice that my heart aches. “Trackers found me, took me in and for that I owe them my unquestioning loyalty.”

Her hands tug at my hair. I can hear in her voice and feel in her touch that her loyalty is not all that unquestioning.

"But I remember family, too. You have to remember those come and gone." She stops to pick up something else to weave into my hair. She has a pile of brightly colored cloth and even metallic copper wire. She pauses, and I turn my head to see her caress a medallion hanging from a leather thong around her neck. She tucks the medallion back into her shirt and pushes my head forward again.

"I'm sorry about your family." Around me, hot water bubbles. It would be relaxing if drinking it wouldn't kill me. I wish I had more to offer Bird.

She gives a sigh and goes back to my hair. "Been a long time. I went through choice when I was just small. No point dwelling on past losses."

With a pat to my head, she stands. "You can't see what it looks like, but it looks good. All twisty and braidy. You look more like a Rogue."

"Thank you. Can I get out now?"

She helps me out. New cloth has been set out for me—fine, soft leather pants and shirt and boots. She helps me dress. With a nod, she starts out the door, but before she goes more than two steps, she turns back to look at me, a hard frown tugging her eyebrows together. She almost looks as if she drank some of the spring water.

She shakes her head and looks as though she isn't sure she wants to tell me anything. But she says, her voice low and rushed, "Something's coming, Lib. It's been coming. I don't know what it is, or what it wants, but it's bad."

Her words send a cold chill through me despite the lingering heat of the hot spring. I want to tell her not to worry. Wolf looks after us. But my dreams linger. I can't deny the truth. I know just what she means.

Bird only offers me a weak smile and a nod, and says, "Tonight, we go to the Empties."

* * *

Bird's bad feeling stays with me. I want to think only about the choice I am making. Is it the right one? Is it right only for me, or for all Glitches? Will other Glitches become Rogues after this or see me as betraying them?

And what about my purpose? It tugs on me, digs in like Wolf's knife, twisting and cutting. I'm supposed to find the other Glitches—not become a Rogue. But what if this will help me with that purpose?

The thought doesn't settle the drive to accomplish my purpose.

I wait in the sleeping room, pacing the floor. It's empty right now. My stomach jumps and part of me wants to just tell everyone I was wrong and it can all go back to how it was. But change is a sign of life. I have to change.

And that has me thinking of Conie and how she said growth was a sign of life. She has to grow. I let out a breath and pull in another one.

Footsteps echo down the tunnel. I turn to see Raj step in. He picks his way around the bedding on the floor. This is like when he came to me and asked that I go with him toward the Norm.

When he reaches me, he folds his arms around himself as if he doesn't know what to do with them. "You're really going through with this? Making the choice?"

I nod. "Yes. It feels right."

He frowns. "But are you really thinking this through? You want to give up what you are?"

"This isn't about giving anything up. I'm taking on something more."

Raj shakes his head. "You're going to end up nothing—not a Glitch and not really a Rogue. Is that really what you want?"

"Why are you saying that? It's not like that. Bird made the choice."

"She was a Rogue to start. But you…you know Wolf doesn't trust us. None of the Rogues do. We're different."

I stiffen. "And that's bad. Now you sound like the AI."

He winces, but I don't care. He is just trying to stop this. "Raj, maybe this is good. Maybe it's good for me. And I know Wolf trusts me."

He sighs and rubs a hand over his face. I know this is the opposite of what he wanted, but I won't change my mind. He must realize he won't stop this because he gives a short nod and turns to one side. He gives me a last lingering look and walks away, his head down and his shoulders slumped. I reach out. I want to stop him—I want to make him understand. I want to tell him I will keep my promise.

Later.

I close my hand on empty air. I can't bring Raj back, so I cling to the one thing that is the only thing I care about right now. Wolf trusts me.

And I trust him that I really can choose to be a Tracker.

* * *

Choice happens at night, but we leave early in the morning.

"Day's journey," Bobcat says. Five Rogues come with me and she happens to be one of them. I hope this means she trusts me, too. Bird and Wolf come with us, but I do not recognize the two other Rogues.

We walk to the ATs and then drive past the hills, through the canyons and out onto the flat lands. The mountains grow closer and larger until they change from blue to tan and green. We stop and cover the ATs. I ask Wolf why we can't take the ATs the whole way.

"Tradition," Wolf tells me. "Rogues once walked out of the Empties. We only go back walking in."

I nod, but I have no idea what that means. Flutters roll around in my stomach. But as long as Wolf is here I know I will be fine.

We set off again, walking single file and keeping quiet. Everyone watches the sky, but the drones don't seem to come here.

The mountains grow larger, but as the sun sinks low I see they aren't mountains. They're too straight and too angular. Metal juts up now from the vague shapes into specific ones. The Empties glitter and shimmer in the dying sun.

"The Empties," Bird whispers and nudges me with an elbow.

It still takes time to really reach the Empties. It isn't until dark that I can look up and see towering castles of glass and marble and metal. Up close, they look… destroyed.

It's obvious the structures were made. Steel and glass come together to form towers where beacons, mostly broken and mangled, sit at the very top to catch the last rays of sunlight. The buildings almost look like skeletons now, their framework exposed from years of being stripped away by the elements. Glass is broken and dirty, steel is half eaten by rust and erosion. And as we walk down a road of hardened black tar, I finally understand why they call it what they do.

A word comes to me from the data orb I touched—city. This was once a city, vast and whole and busy.

Now it's utterly empty. No wonder they call it the Empties.

It is silent, too, save for Wolf's deep, quiet voice. "This is one of the last places, from a time before the domes rose and before the AI. This is where our people gathered and lived—some say in peace. Others say in war. The storm came and swallowed it up and the people fled. The Rogues walked away. We walked as we walk back. But the Empties stand. They go on. Like the Rogues. Now they wait here, silent and empty, for caretakers that will one day return."

Wolf turns to me. I can only gaze back. I feel like I've just been told about the creation of the universe. In a way, I have.

"Lib of the Glitches. We, the Tracker Clan, bring you here on this night to have you choose as the Rogues once chose. Prove your worth and your loyalty. Search out the good left in the

Empties. See the past so you know where the Rogues began, and if it is your choice to walk with us, come to us and walk this Earth as one with the Tracker clan."

His eyes seem impossibly dark. I feel as if I could get lost in them. I cannot summon words, but it seems a nod is all that is required of me.

Bobcat gives a nod. She and Wolf each take one hand and lead me into the dead city. Bird whispers a curt warning. "Be careful."

I stay close to Wolf and Bobcat. The others seem to be waiting for us back at the edge of the city.

"This is a scavenge," Bobcat says in a hushed tone. Rubble crunches under my boots. They are the new boots given to me and I wish I didn't have to get them dirty, but I do as we walk through the Empties. The buildings around us seem to have been set up in a grid, the lines and corners looking like they form perfect angles and squares, though it's difficult to really see that from the ground.

"Scavenge for what exactly?" I ask.

She shrugs. "Anything useful."

"Parts," Wolf says. He lets go of my hand to shift the pouch he wears slung over one shoulder. Bobcat wears a pouch, too, as do I. "Pieces for the ATs. Metal for knives. Fixings for the solar panels. And things our people may have once left behind."

I glance at Bobcat. She looks only half interested in any of this, and it makes me wonder how many times she's done this.

"Why do you care about what was left? Wouldn't it have been left because it wasn't needed?"

The corner of his mouth twitches. "If we know our past, we can strive to not repeat it. There is too much we don't know—too much the AI swallowed up and wouldn't tell. We don't know what ended the Empties and made them into this." He waves a hand at the ruined buildings.

Thinking about the data orb, I nod. The AI knows what happened but doesn't seem to want to share the data. What did happen? Could it happen again? With a shiver, I straighten and keep walking. And start really looking.

We spend the whole night in the Empties. It was a long trip to get here and I didn't sleep much the night before. I try not to stumble. I'm sure I'm dragging—and not seeing anything because of it. If anyone notices, they don't mention it…

The third building we head into almost falls on us. The next one seems to have been some sort of housing for vehicles.

"Most of these use fossil fuels," Bobcat explains. "Petrochemical—you can tell 'cause they still stink. They aren't very useful. But some of the parts—like the wheels—work on ATs."

She heads to one of the vehicles. Its tires are long gone, but she tears it open and digs, pulling out wires that are partially rotted.

When she waves at me, I head over and she points at a tube. “That one. Go ahead and take it.”

Biting my lip, I try tugging it out. It’s stuck. Bobcat pulls out a knife and hands it to me. She grins. “Don’t know a Rogue who doesn’t need a knife. Keep it.”

Wetting my lips, I pry loose the part. When I offer it to her, she grins and shoves it into my bag. “That’s how we do it.”

We spend the rest of the evening taking bolts or bits of metal. Sometimes we find chunks of round, dull metal, and Wolf says, “We can remake the metal into parts and knives.”

I find the Empties sad. Now and then I will step into a room and see a broken seat, or an image that shows a family group, or the wind will lift and cry through the dying buildings. Despite what Wolf said earlier, I do not think anyone is ever going to come back here. Conie would never allow it. And why would anyone want to? This place makes the tunnels seem close and safe.

When the sun lifts again and touches the tips of the broken towers, Wolf leads the way back to the others. Bobcat keeps an eye on the sky, but I don’t think a drone would ever come here. This is a place to ignore.

I am exhausted, but I walk with the others back to the ATs. I glance back once at the Empties. It is so sad that the Rogues once had to walk away—and do so again. But I glance at Wolf and see only determination.

I ride back behind Wolf, holding onto him. Am I a Tracker now?

I am ready to drop once we get into the tunnels. I walk into the main room but have to blink. It seems everyone is here. Even the Glitches stand off to one side. The room erupts with shouts and stomping boots.

Wolf claps a hand on my shoulder, and I look up at him. His face is grim, but his eyes are warm and almost seem to whisper to me.

You belong now.

"The clan has grown," Wolf calls out.

I glance around, smiling, but my stomach knots. I can feel Raj's stare on me. I hope the Rogues won't regret this. I hope no one will.

Chapter Twenty-One

The celebration goes on until night comes again. I am already tired, but the lack of sleep leaves me giddy and I don't want this day to end. Extra food is brought out. Drums come out as well, and the Rogues dance, eat and tell stories. Bobcat challenges another Rogue to wrestle, and everyone cheers when she pins a man twice her weight. Rogues come over and slap my back or offer me water or food. I want to burst into tears. Good ones.

Thankfully, Wolf stays by my side.

He leans close to whisper in my ear, "Like being a Rogue?"

I blush hot, grin and nod. "Yes!" With a laugh, I spin with my arms out.

Wolf watches me and shakes his head. But he grabs me around the waist to twirl me around.

Dizzy, I cling to his shoulders. Pleasure washes over me and through me. It's wonderful.

Everything is perfect, except for a whisper in the back of my mind that tells me I'm wrong.

I try not to give it any attention, but I can feel Bird watching me. She sits at the very edge of the Rogues and watches me with dark, narrowed eyes. I think I see worry in her eyes—and something darker.

Something's coming, Lib. Something's been coming.

I try to shove it aside, but now that I've seen it, I can't help but see the rest, too.

The Glitches sit with their backs to the walls, looking like outcasts. Chandra and Marq never seem interested in what's going on around them, so I'm not surprised to see them keeping to themselves. But Skye is watching the Rogues with a small, pained smile. And Raj—he has his back to me.

When Wolf finally puts me back on the ground, he is laughing and I hang onto him. I don't want to pull away. But now I've seen Raj and Skye. I cannot ignore the looks upon their faces.

I look up at Wolf and tell him, "I'll be right back." I don't want to tell him that I'm going to check on Skye and Raj, but he will see what I do. There is no way to hide anything in the tunnels.

He frowns, but he nods. And he cups my cheek with one hand.

A thrill runs through me. Wolf steps back from me and watches as I head over to Skye and Raj. I grab a plate with meat on it and finally make it over to Skye.

I sit down next to her, but Raj instantly stands. He gives me a cool look that leaves me chilled, turns and disappears down one of the tunnels.

I turn back to Skye and hold out the plate of meat.

She takes a chunk and lifts one shoulder. "He's just like that sometimes."

I don't think this is just Raj being Raj. But Skye doesn't want to talk about it, and I don't want to ask. For an awkward moment, neither of us says anything.

Skye eats the meat, swallows and asks, "So…you're with the Rogues now?" Her voice is monotone and her eyes distant. She stares past me.

I frown. "You're with them, too, you know."

She forces a smile. It looks strangely mechanical. My stomach knots. "Yes, right here in the same room. I just—" She shrugs. "The Norm was so much nicer. It was easier. I…I miss my family. I miss—" She breaks off, unable to finish. She only shakes her head.

I know what she was going to say. She misses everything. I understand why. I remember the green grass and the cool air and the sense that everyone had enough food and water and a purpose in life.

I have one too, and it is gnawing at me

Just as quickly, I remember how Raj narrowly escaped that place. Conie manipulated the Techs, reprogrammed them to do terrible things—controlled them. Maybe the Norm is easier, but I'm not sure it's better.

"But you're here now. Why not enjoy the now?" I ask.

Skye flashes another dull smile and takes a piece of meat. She doesn't eat it.

Biting my lip, I search for something that is honest. Finally, I say in a quiet voice, "I'm glad you're here. I wouldn't have made it without you."

Skye looks at me and puts her hand over mine. But then she pulls it away and says, "You'd better go back to your new place."

Chapter Twenty-Two

Life shifts. In some ways for the better and some not. My sleeping arrangements change, though just barely. Skye sleeps next to Chandra and Bird sleeps as far from me as she can. Bobcat seems to take pity on me and sometimes sleeps nearby. Some of the Rogues will eat and talk with me.

But only some.

At meals, I never know if I should eat with Rogues or Glitches. Raj won't eat with me, and so I start to avoid the Glitches, but not all Rogues will stay if I sit down. I can eat with Croc or Bobcat. I haven't dared to sit beside Wolf during meals. He is their leader and those he sits with never change, but I catch his gaze on me often during meals.

Maybe it is only my imagination that he wants me to sit with him. I can't tell anymore.

Mostly, I think things are better. My days are busy. The Rogues teach me to work metal and I can hunt with them. But I still have horrible dreams and a whisper that is telling me I'm not doing the right thing. I'm not fulfilling my purpose. It's going to go wrong, and it's all my fault.

I wake sweating and shaking, and some days I just wish I could be temporarily nonfunctional without dreams. And I have no one I can really talk to.

Skye will smile at me, but she stays with the other Glitches. She doesn't ask me to go with her on a connect. I'm hurt and a little angry. Why are they acting like this? They could choose to join the clan, too.

I'm thinking about this as I stride down the tunnel toward the main room when I hear voices. Wolf's deep, rumbling tones stand out. The other sounds like Lion, a Rogue who has made it clear he doesn't like me. Lion is one of those who avoids me. I slow my steps.

Lion's voice rises and I hear him say, "…walks around like she owns the place!"

A lump sticks in my throat. I'm certain he is complaining about me.

Wolf answers in a low growl. "Lib is clan."

"She's still a Glitch. You don't think she's like the others? Willing to go back to the Norm if she could? She's a broken Tech."

"Enough!" Wolf sounds angry. I stop where I am, my palms damp and my heart pounding against my ribs so hard it's making me sick.

Lion doesn't listen. His voice lifts louder. "What makes her so damn special? Everyone sees the way you look at her. You don't look at her like she's a Glitch. You don't seem to remember what—"

"Enough," Wolf says in a quiet voice that raises bumps on my skin.

Lion's voice drops to a sulky tone. "Someone's gotta say it."

I glance behind me. Should I leave? I want to get closer to see if Wolf is defending me or really defending himself. But I don't want them to know I've heard anything.

Before I can decide, Wolf says, his voice cold as night, "Fine. Say it."

I hear Lion's boots shift on the dirt and then he says, "Everyone talks about how you ignore Bird now. The clan thinks she's the right one to lead at your side, and now you barely notice her."

The lump moves from my throat to my stomach. Bird—Wolf and Bird. My skin chills. Didn't Skye once say that Wolf and Bird were supposed to be together? I know Wolf does look at me in a way he hasn't looked at anyone else.

But maybe I want something I have no right to want.

Wolf's boots also scuffle the dirt. "What is between me and Bird is between me and Bird. That's none of your concern."

“It is a concern to the clan if you plan to put a Glitch at your side. You think the clan will ever follow a Glitch? It’ll break the clan if you give her a place at your side.”

I turn away and start down the tunnel, moving away from Wolf and Lion. I don’t want to hear any more. My stomach burns. So does my face. Now I know what the rest of the clan thinks. I may have chosen to join them, but they have a choice, too. And some will never accept me.

With my eyes down on the dark ground, I almost run into Bobcat. She puts out a hand and I stop in front of her. She gives me a crooked smile. “Lib, there you are. You want to go out with us tomorrow on a scavenge? I’ve gotten stuck with Chandra the last two times and I can’t stand her and her staring off into the distance like all she can think about is getting back into the Norm.”

I glance back over my shoulder and see Wolf now. His shoulders look tense as if he’s braced himself. Our stares meet, his dark and intense and filled with something that might be uncertainty. Does he know I heard him and Lion?

“Lib, did you hear?” Bobcat asks, putting a hand on my shoulder.

My face and hands turn cold. Wolf frowns and turns away. It sounds as if Bobcat knows what I heard, but she doesn’t. However, Wolf knows. I see it in his face before he turns. It feels as if a knife blade sticks into my ribs. I turn to face Bobcat. Getting away from here seems a good idea right now.

*   *   *

The next day it is not just me on the scavenge. Raj goes, too. It is not just a routine scavenge. We're going to the Empties. Raj glances at me when he sees me, but he gives me a nod. At least he is not going to refuse to be with me.

Bobcat is leading. Wolf has other things to do. Disappointment curls inside me, but I'm also relieved. I don't have to pretend I didn't hear Lion tell Wolf I shouldn't be clan. And if Wolf was here, Raj might refuse to go with us. Lion is also not going and I am glad of that. Now I want to avoid him the way he avoids me and that's hard, given how small the group is and how we have to be in the main room for meals.

The trip is long—just like always. We leave the ATs outside the Empties and walk. On the way, I ask Bobcat, "I thought going to the Empties was just for special days?"

Bobcat shakes her head. "The choice is tradition. The Empties are a resource. Yes, all of Wolf's story is true. The Rogues once walked out of the Empties, and we walk back on special days. But the Empties have things we can use. We can't ignore that."

I nod. "Waste nothing. That's law."

Bobcat tells everyone to spread out. Six of us are on the scavenge. I'm paired with Raj and am surprised when Bobcat doesn't tell another Rogue to come with us. When Mouse says something about this, Bobcat waves a hand. "Lib's clan. No point wasting manpower on a babysitting job."

A spark of pride warms me, but Raj scowls and takes off without me, walking fast and keeping ahead of me. I have to hurry to catch up.

The roads are hard in the Empties. It's not rock and not dirt and I wonder what the people who built the Empties used. I ask Raj, but he just shrugs. So I say, "I haven't seen a platform. Do you know where we can connect?"

Raj spares me a glance and says in a tired voice, "There aren't any. The Empties were built before the AI existed. Didn't they tell you that? Or do they still keep things from you like they do other Glitches?"

The bitterness is biting, but at least he's speaking to me. "I forgot," I admit and bite the inside of my cheek.

He snorts and strides ahead. I hurry again to keep up. The wind doesn't sing through the metal. I don't see birds or other animals here. I smell only dust. The Empties really are empty of life. I no longer hear the steps of the other Rogues. It's just Raj's boots and my quiet steps. I cannot walk as silently as a Rogue, but I no longer make as much noise as a Glitch.

Glancing into another building that is filled with rubble, I ask, "Then what are we doing here if we're not going to connect?"

"Didn't they explain?"

Annoyance tightens in my chest. I roll my eyes. "I know how to scavenge. But why take Glitches to the Empties?"

Raj stops and whirls around to face me. The pulse beats in his tightened jaw. He looks like he's about to yell at me.

But he frowns and asks in a quiet voice, "You still consider yourself one of us? You still think of yourself as a Glitch?"

I lift both hands and hold them out at my sides. "Of course I'm a Glitch. Nothing can change that." I bite down on my lower lip. I don't want to think about what else I might be—what the AI might have done to me. I don't even want to think about that.

Raj seems to study my face. Slowly, a smile tugs on his lips. Warmth floods me. I hope we can repair our friendship. Maybe.

"We're looking for scraps, same as everyone. But Glitches have an advantage. We know what gear looks like. We've seen it in the Norm. Most of this stuff is too outdated to use, but some of it is worth taking back. Every now and then you'll find a circuit that can still hold power. Very rarely you'll find an old handheld—and we can use that to help with—" He breaks off and shoots me a sideways glance as if he's nervous about something.

He clears his throat. "It's a scavenge. We just also happen to be smarter about what's really useful gear."

I smile and shake my head. "Smarter? So that's why we get stuck with more work."

His lips twitch. But I'm not really joking. Glitches seem much smarter than Rogues, and I wonder if the AI does something to Techs to limit or change our processing ability. But I don't want to ruin this moment and the tentative return of this friendship.

Raj starts walking again, but this time he keeps his pace to one that I can easily match.

As we move through the Empties, I watch Raj sort through gear. He picks up anything with wires. Some of the gear he tosses aside, but some he puts into the pouch he wears. I don't recognize any of it, but I notice he keeps any handheld device, even if the screen is cracked. He also digs through the rubble, pulling out circuit boards that are similar to the paneling on a platform. Sometimes the boards have raised keys and unfamiliar markings. He grabs cords and shiny rocks that he tells me are rubies. "You can use these to make a laser—you know, create coherent light. That's what the drones have and use as weapons."

I nod and think of the hot beam that came out of the drone to kill an animal. I am not sure anyone should have a laser. As Raj gathers gear, I start to notice none of this would be valued by Rogues.

They search for gear to repair the ATs and keep them working, and to make knifes. Raj collects gear that could be useful in the Norm—computer parts really. Nothing mechanical.

Raj's pouch doesn't seem full. Most of what he has are small components. I have the same. We start back to the point where we will meet the others and I ask, "What is this for?" I keep my voice quiet. I don't want the others to hear.

Raj shrugs casually, but I can see the tension in his shoulders. He doesn't look at me when he answers. "It's gear. To help with the drones, remember? But…when we get back. Let's stash this where the Glitches sit. We've got work to do before any of this gear can be useful, and I don't want the Rogues tossing it as being not useful or melting it down to make a stupid knife."

I nod as if I agree. However, I'm not sure I believe him.

I'm also not sure what this gear can do, but I have ideas. Thinking about it, I know I could construct a power supply. Chemicals coupled with the copper wiring and a metallic conductor would work. And the rubies to create the coherent light. That is for a weapon.

Or an advanced connect to core systems within the AI that would let Raj hack the system.

I don't tell Raj any of this. I'm unwilling to start an argument with him, and this could lead to a weapon to use against the drones. A much better weapon than rocks. But the weapon could also be used on Techs inside the Norm to get to the AI. I don't like that idea.

I decide I'll need to watch Raj. I fear there is only one reason he wants this gear.

He still thinks he can fix the AI.

I know nothing can.

Chapter Twenty-Three

I am not thinking about Raj or the AI as I duck to one side. Wolf's fist sails past my head. Using the momentum, I spin and come up behind Wolf. This is a good opportunity to set him on his ass, but I only tap his thigh with my boot to let him know that I am there and could do more.

He swivels around and narrows his eyes at me as if he is going to throw another punch, but the effect is lost when I catch the curve of his mouth, tipping up into a smile.

Sparring every day is building my strength and speed, but today something shifts between us. I stare at Wolf, my breathing hard and he stares back. My heart races in a way that is odd. I don't really have a word for it, no frame of reference, but I can sense this moment is significant. It is important. I am aware of Wolf in a different way—as if my body is attuned to his. As if I can feel what he feels. Something happens in my chest. It is as if my heart gives an odd twist. It is so unexpected it shocks me into standing still and simply staring at Wolf.

Slowly, Wolf straightens and tells me, his voice oddly rough, "You shouldn't tease."

I flash a small smile. "You mean just go ahead and knock you flat?"

He lifts an eyebrow. His move comes fast. He launches himself at me. I try to duck, but he anticipates the move and catches me around the waist. The air whooshes out as I hit the dirt. Wolf rolls once with me, ending up on top. He pins my arms to the sand and for a moment I am stunned. Then he grins.

Suddenly all I can feel is how his hips rest against mine. How his hands feel on my wrists, pressed against my skin. Something instinctual stirs inside me. Heat flashes up from between my legs and into my belly. I am tingling and out of breath. I process my body's reaction and respond without any input from my brain.

I want him to be even closer than he is.

With my heart wildly thumping, my skin flushed, my chest rising and falling fast, I keep my gaze locked on his.

His expression shifts and softens until his smile is small and gentle. Slowly, that smile fades and a look of hunger comes into his eyes. He leans down toward me, as if he, too, wants to be closer than we are. Heat from his body washes over me and the scent of his musky sweat and something that is unique to him wraps around me. I like his scent. His face hovers over mine. His breath brushes my cheek and then my lips.

His gaze flickers down over my body and up again, seeming to ask a silent question I don't understand and don't know how to answer. All I can do is part my lips and then lick the lower one.

The corner of his mouth lifts and he puts his lips on mine. I am lost in a sense of power and electrical heat, unlike anything I've ever felt. My eyes flutter closed. The jolt tingles on my skin and surges through my entire body, that single point of contact and I—

"Wolf!" Lion shouts the word. It jars me out of the moment.

As though prodded by a stick in his back, Wolf jerks up and jumps to his feet. His dark skin is tinged with red. He doesn't look at me. Turning, he brushes off his pants and holds out a hand to me. I'm dazed enough that I only stare at it.

But then Lion is here at the training ground. He ignores me. "Wolf, you're needed. The scavenge went bad." Lion leans over and braces his hands on his knees. He has been running and barely gets the words out. Wolf is already running. Lion turns and follows. I climb to my feet and follow, my head spinning and now with the back of my neck tingling. This is not good. Lion's face, pale and strained tells me that much.

Back in the tunnels, I head to the main room. It seems like everyone is here, but Croc is here and looking pale, too. Skye crouches on the ground, her arms around herself, and is rocking back and forth. I don't see Bird, and that kicks my pulse up even faster than it was before.

I take a deep breath to slow my heartbeat and look around.

Two Rogues stand over another who lies on the floor. Marq sits by himself, far away from everyone, hunched over as if he wants to disappear. It is odd not to see Chandra with him. Two other Rogues stand with their hands over their faces. Lion glances at me, eyes narrow and hot, and I almost take a step back. That look is filled with hate.

"What's going on?" I ask Mole, who stands nearest to me. She looks up, her eyes brimming with moisture. She turns away without saying anything.

Wolf's booming voice echoes my question. "What happened?"

Croc puts one hand on Skye's trembling shoulders. Her face looks as if she covered it with white ash from a fire. Croc says something, his voice so low I can't make out the words. He looks grim, his mouth set into a thin, angry line after he speaks.

"How?" Wolf says, the one word sharp and cold.

Skye looks up. Her pale face makes her eyes look bigger, but they, too, are paler than I remember—a blue that looks like the sky in the cold morning. Her stare finds me and lingers with something I can only describe as fear.

Others glance at me now, too. Rogues turn to glare at me with their stony, accusing stares.

Something tugs at my arm. I glance over and find Raj pulling at my arm. I go with him and he pulls me away from the others. But I glance back at the Rogue who lies on the ground.

The Rogue isn't lying there to nap or because of an injury. The head rests at an angle and the open, blank eyes are like those I have seen in dreams. This Rogue is forever nonfunctional. She is going to go back into the ground.

Bobcat is no more.

My skin chills and my stomach clenches. For a moment I fear that what I last ate will come up again. It doesn't, but a sour taste fills my mouth. Now I am trembling just like Skye.

Raj leads me over to where Marq crouches and sits down. I sit with them. The Rogues turn away from me. I blink and wipe at the moisture in my eyes. How can Bobcat be nonfunctional? How can this be happening?

Chapter Twenty-Four

In a quiet voice, Raj tells us what happened.

"I wasn't on the scavenge, but Bobcat went out with Chandra and Skye."

Marq nods as if he knows this. Raj glances at him and then puts his stare on the rock wall opposite us. Eight went out. Five made it back. Bobcat, Snake and Chandra didn't make it. Horse and Tiger brought Bobcat back, but she didn't make it. Not really."

"Skye?" I ask, glancing over to her. She sits holding herself and I can't tell if she is hurt badly or not.

Raj glances over to Skye, too. "By what I saw, injured, but she should be able to self-repair. Croc won't let me get close enough to her to tell. When I glance over, Croc's gaze darts away from mine.

My mouth dries. It is not unheard of to go back into the ground in the Outside. I learned that the day Bear did not come back to the tunnels. But I have forgotten how unforgiving the Outside can be.

"What happened?" I ask Raj. I put my hands in my lap. Marq shakes his head and turns away as if he doesn't want to hear anything else.

Raj sighs. "Horse was babbling when they came back. Said it caught them off guard." He stops and glances around as if looking for who might be listening. But everyone else is over with Wolf and listening to Horse and Tiger tell the story. Mole sits on the ground next to Bobcat, stroking her hair.

I look at Raj. "What did you hear?"

He makes a face and says, his voice grim, "A drone."

The words spike cold down my back. I remember the hum—and seeing a drone kill. I swallow.

Raj lowers his voice. "They haven't been out during the day in a long time. Tiger said they were heading for one of the old platforms. Horse said no one was watching the sky." He frowns as though he's not sure he believes this.

Shaking my head, I tell him, "Bobcat would have been careful."

He shakes his head. "Maybe it's just the drones are changing schedules. Or maybe the AI was waiting for them. The AI doesn't leave things to chance."

I nod. Raj is right. We fall silent and sit, watching the others. It seems to me that Wolf is listening to the other Rogues and not saying much. But he looks up. I see both anger and worry in his eyes. The same knots my insides.

*   *   *

For three sleep cycles, Wolf will not send anyone out on scavenge. But water is running low. It's always top priority to bring in more. I volunteer to go. I hear from Croc that Skye is still repairing. Marq is more withdrawn than ever and I worry he is not eating enough. No one seems to care. Raj and I avoid the others.

Bobcat is put back into the ground. The Rogues go out at night to do this. I am not asked to go with them. Bird sits with Mouse and Mole and tells Bobcat's story so they will remember. I go to Croc to ask what he has tried to make the water in the hot springs something we can drink. He tells me he has no time to talk to me. I go away with my face stinging and my head down. It is the first time Croc has acted like this to me.

Unable to sit and do nothing, I go to Wolf to tell him I will go on the next scavenge. I can connect and hack for water better than anyone.

Wolf answers me with a slash of his hand and a shake of his head. We no longer train in the mornings and I miss it. I miss him. I want to ask if we can meet tomorrow morning, but my courage is fluid and slips away before I can grasp and hold it.

Wolf glances at me and says, "Marq and Raj will scavenge." He starts to turn away, but before he does, he reaches out with one finger and touches the back of my hand. He pulls away at once. Worry still haunts his eyes, and that leaves me worried as well.

I tell Raj to be careful—very careful. I remember my dark dreams where death fills these tunnels and leaves everyone nonfunctional. I cannot look at Bird without thinking of her warning. Bird avoids me, as do the other Rogues. I wonder what happened to Chandra. Was she left for the animals to eat? I shudder at that. The faces of the dead flash through my mind. They taunt me, accuse me.

It's all my fault.

Part of me believes that.

And part of me wonders if it is really the AI's fault? Is the AI really a glitched system?

Waiting for those out to scavenge is hard. This is worse than when Bear didn't come back. I think everyone is thinking the same thing. Are the drones more dangerous now?

Skye is no longer being cared for by Croc and comes to sit with me. She will not talk about what happened, but she is also not eating much. She is thinner than she once was. And she is still pale.

I hear the shout first. It is too much like before when Lion yelled for Wolf.

Standing, I tell Skye, "Stay here." I head toward the tunnel where I hear boots hitting the ground and the sounds of disaster.

Fear quivers inside me. I am truly afraid of what I will see. Will Raj's face be too pale, his eyes glassy and unseeing? Or Marq? Or Bird? Or Bull who went out? Or Lion?

I try to tell myself I have to hope, but it all seems so useless. I can't believe in anything. I must see they are still functional.

Eight went out again. Two stagger back into the main room—Lion and Bull. I can't swallow, my throat is too tight. No bodies come back this time. Those who pull themselves into the main room are covered in what looks like red mud. I know better. It is blood and dirt. The faces look strained, their eyes glassy as if they cannot even understand what happened.

Wolf strides in and sends Mouse and Bird to get water for these two. I glance around. I hear more footsteps in the tunnels and I stare into the darkness. Are there more? Please let more come back.

My heart seems to beat with dull, heavy thuds. I worry I will not see Raj again, that he, like Chandra, will have been left for the animals to eat. That he—

"We never stood a chance." It's Raj's voice. He strides down the tunnel into the main room. He's alive.

I throw my arms around him. Stepping back, I hang onto him. I want to feel his warm skin, to make certain he is not damaged in a way beyond repair.

From behind him, Bird steps into the room. Her ribbons flare wildly around her head. She's in front of me in an instant. I have time only to blink, and then she shoves at me hard enough to send me to the ground.

"You!" she screams, her voice shaking and moisture in her eyes. "This is your fault!"

My eyes go wide. I want to shake my head and tell her she is wrong. This is all wrong. But my dreams tell me different. The AI did not send Techs after me, the way it did with Raj. The AI wants me to find the Glitches. What if I have found them all here?

It can't be. It's not my fault. It's not—

Even as I say it over and over in my head, I realize I might be wrong. Looking up, I see that no one is saying anything to contradict Bird. No one defends me. Not Raj, who looks as if he is in shock. Not Wolf, who does not look at me.

But Skye's voice lifts, small and shaky. "Lib wouldn't betray us! She's a good person."

"She's a Glitch." I glance over. Lion stares back at me. But angry mutters rise.

Bird stares at me. "She dreams of death. She dreams we're all dead."

I let out a long slow breath. I can't deny that. And Lion calls out, "What if she's calling the drones? What if the AI sent her to find us?"

I glance around. Everyone seems to be staring at me, even Raj and Skye.

Lion mutters, "Glitches—there's always something wrong with them."

Looking at Skye, I see her flinch at the insult that hits not just me, but her and Raj, too. Lifting my chin, I raise my voice. "What about Marq? He didn't come back. And Chandra. You think a Glitch would take out another Glitch?"

Lion shrugs. "Why not. The AI threw you out to waste in the Outside. You were already dead when we found you."

I step back as if Lion has struck me. He thinks I'd be fine with not just Rogues dying, but Glitches made permanently nonfunctional, too?

I can't help the urge. I look over at Wolf. He'll defend me. He knows I'm not bad. He trusts me.

He meets my stare, but there is nothing welcoming in his eyes. He seems the Wolf I first met—hard and inflexible. A solid wall of distrust slaps me down.

When he speaks, his voice is cold and even. “As leader of this clan, I call for council.” His dark eyes glitter with some emotion I can’t understand. “We decide Lib’s fate.”

I put my head down. I know that means nothing good for me.

Chapter Twenty-Five

The council is made of nine Rogues—and me. I follow the others down one of the darkest, narrowest tunnels and step into a small room with a single hole overhead that lets in a strong shaft of light. I am told to stand under the light. It is strong enough to warm my skin. Bird is here, as is Wolf and Lion. I know Bobcat should be here. And two more. Stones are set around the room as seats, and three are left empty. Three who have died in the two scavenges gone wrong.

I don't think that is going to help me.

I want Skye and Raj to be here and I ask for that.

Wolf shakes his head. His long, dark hair sways a little. "No Glitches—except you. You are allowed because you must stand before council."

I look around. Mouse's mother is here, an older woman who is probably in her late twenties. Her name is Wind and I know she came to the Trackers from another clan, like Bird did. She looks at the others, not at me as she speaks. "This one has brought us uncertainty and chaos. She is wrong in a way we have not seen before."

Hands clenched at my sides, I shake my head. "Wrong how? What have I to do with drones? I haven't done anything wrong." The words taste strangely like a lie, but it's the truth. I know it is.

Wind ignores me. "Six have gone back into the ground, including Bear, since this Glitch came. Do we keep on with this until the whole clan is no more?"

The others swap glances. They sit in a semicircle in front of me. Bird stares at her hands, her head lowered and the blood still on her arms. She rubs her palms together. Her words about my dreams are the most damaging thing against me, but I don't know what to say.

"Law says we think first of the clan." This comes from Horse, a man who only looks a couple of years older than Wolf. "This Glitch brings bad luck. We cannot have that."

"Remember, she is clan," Wolf says, his voice soft.

I glance at him. His face doesn't look soft. I can't hope for help from him.

"What evidence do we have she has done wrong?" A woman named Elk straightens and pushes back her hair. She has a kind voice and could be any age. Her dark skin is unlined and her brown eyes seem sad. "We cannot just cast her out without evidence."

"She's a Glitch before she's anything else," Horse says. He folds his arms over his chest. "Law is we don't waste, but this is worse than if she's no use."

Elk shakes her head. "She's clan." A silence falls. No one will meet my eyes.

I wet my lips and say, "I am clan. I chose. I joined the Trackers. Has any Glitch done that before?" No one answers. "Well, doesn't that prove something? That I am here to be of use—that I can help?" I look around at the grim faces staring at me. I realize this is no help to me. In the end, I am still only a Glitch.

I am different.

Wolf frowns, but Bird looks up and says, "I am Bird Sees Far. My clan was gifted with sight for those who trained in how to use it, and I tell you the truth now. I have the sight, and those of you who know me know my visions are never wrong, even if they are not always clear."

Heads nod, and a few mutter approval of this. I turn my stare at Bird. Visions. The word pings in my brain and connects. It is an uncanny ability to see either the future or events beyond ordinary sight. This is how Bird came across me and Raj. She saw us.

"What do your visions show?" Elk asks.

Bird looks at each person and then puts her gaze on me. Her eyes glow hot with anger—and fear. "I see the smoke of ruins. I see Lib walking in shadows. She is something…something odd. I thought she would do great things—and she will. But now I see more. I see a valley of death. She brings destruction with her. She will change the world, and may mercy be upon us when she does for it will forever alter every path of every living thing. And I see a link, a tie between her and the AI. She is sheltered by the AI. She is used by our enemy."

The room stills. Bird's voice fills me with a terrible dread. A certainty settles inside my chest like a weight. I don't want this to be true. But there are threads of truth.

It's all my fault.

But can I change that? A vision is simply a sign. It is not yet fact.

However, glances slip away from me. Those who look at me do so with mouths thinned and eyes dark and cold. Bird has made up their minds about me. I dare not look at Wolf. I don't want to know what he thinks of me now, but my gaze slips to him.

His eyes are dark and unreadable.

He stands to face me and raises his hand. "We cannot decide in two beats of a heart what one of the clan must endure for the rest of time. Think on this for one cycle of time. For a day and a night. When we return, your fate, Lib, will be decided."

The others file out one at a time. Wolf is the last to go. He stops and stares at me. It reminds me of when we first met and he put me into the Coffin. Now will he put me into the Outside—where I will most certainly end nonfunctional? Or will I? Do I know enough to survive on my own? Or could I go back to the Norm—to the AI—and tell Conie I failed. Would she take me back?

I shudder at the thought. The AI's drones killed Marq and Chandra. They have killed too many Rogues. They will kill the clan if they are allowed. Lifting my chin, I meet Wolf's stare. He gives a nod as if he has decided something. I don't know what it is.

But I have things to think over, too.

Chapter Twenty-Six

The council room dims and stars come out overhead. I stare up at the ceiling. I can't sleep. Sleep brings dreams filled with death that only reminds me there is truth in Bird's words.

I am supposed to do something. I bring destruction with me. But whose? So many have become…I stop there. I hate that phrase nonfunctional. That is a Glitch…no, that is an AI phrase. Death is what comes to any human…and I am human, too.

How can it be my fault if I haven't done anything to help the AI?

But I think of the AI, secure in the Norm and with all her systems in place. How she spoke to me calmly even when she knew I was trying to help Raj all along. She was so familiar to me. She had the face of my mother. I long again to be back in a connect—that world is so much more comfortable than this one.

"No," I whisper to the empty room. "It's not."

Saying the words aloud doesn't chase away the feelings. I sit up and stare at the darkness. My eyes are used to seeing with very little light. I know how to use my hearing to judge where the wall is. I can smell fresh or stale air. Folding my legs up beneath me, I stare at the rock where Wolf sat and wonder how quickly I got here. It seems another life, the one where I was clan. But in so short a time I had. It could almost be a dream. I touch my lips. Even the press of Wolf's mouth to mine seems as if it happened to someone else.

Perhaps it did. Perhaps that was a Lib who forgot her function—her real purpose. It no longer matters what the Rogue council decides. Slow knowledge builds within me. I must leave. I will not stay to allow others to decide my fate.

The AI threw me out of the Norm. I am done with others choosing for me.

But there is more at stake than my own life.

I think of Skye and how I found her facing sentinels in a bad connect. She is thin now and I know she will get thinner. The Outside is hard on her, dangerous and biting. It isn't for a girl like her.

The Norm, however, is. It's so perfect there is no struggle to survive, no scraping and scrounging. No need to hunt for food and no killing heat. Skye could be safe in the Norm. She could be happy. So would Raj. He wants to be with his family again and should be.

But that can't happen with the AI as she is now.

I promised Raj we would go back to reprogram the AI. If I do that, Skye can return to the Norm. She can be happy. Raj can find his family. Maybe I can go back with them. Maybe I will find my mother and all my memories—if they exist. But I am not like Raj and Skye. Bird is right when she says there is something strange about me. I am not really sure I want to know more about myself, but I need to think of Skye and Raj now, and any other Glitches who may be with other Rogue clans.

Standing up quickly, I decide I must go. I will go. I can tell Conie I found the Glitches—and I will find a way to make her take them back as Techs. I will correct the errors.

And maybe I can figure out how she's tracking Rogues, too.

A wild hope lifts that I can return to the Rogues if I do that. I will be welcomed back. Wolf might put his mouth on mine again and press his body close. Or I will die.

I will deal with all that later. Right now, I must escape the tunnels.

Moving as quietly as a Rogue, I stand and quickly head to the main room.

I do not worry about being caught. I worry about being stopped before I can get what I need to make it to the Norm.

That fear makes me move faster. In the main room, I head to where the Glitches sit and pull out my pouch, which still has the gear from the scavenge that Raj and I did in the Empties. I'm going to miss him, but I don't let that thought slow me down. If this works, I'll see him again. Maybe in the Norm.

With my pouch strap slung over my head and sitting crossways on my body, I head to the storage room, a short tunnel that is just off the main room. I grab one skin with water and a handful of dried meat. I glance around. Croc keeps his dry plant for healing in his room, but the storage room holds cloth, food that is dried or salted to keep, barrels of water, and even the seeds Raj and I scavenged that haven't yet been put into the ground to grow. Everything for the clan to survive. It seems so little.

I don't want to take from the clan, but I must. They are wrong about one thing—the clan needs to think more about each individual. The clan couldn't go on without Wolf…but it will go on without me.

Before I go, I remember the cold outside and take a single jacket of thick, black cloth. I hope it will help me blend in with the darkness. I pull it on and head for one of the exit tunnels, lifting my head to smell the cold clean air.

I have no idea what awaits me in the Norm, but I know the AI will be awake. And maybe Conie is waiting for me.

Chapter Twenty-Seven

The desert is cold. The jacket is too big for me, the sleeves too long, but that means I can tuck my fingers up into the sleeves for added warmth. I walk for almost an hour before I think it is safe enough to stop and rest. Mindful of the creatures that will be out—I can hear their scenting and their howls and sometimes their padding paws tracking me—I find an outcropping of rocks and check it thoroughly before I sit down.

I drink two sips of water, eat one bite of meat, and then settle to do the real work.

I unpack the items scavenged from the Empties. My lips are dry and I want another sip of water, but I resist the urge to drink. I have to use only what I need when I need it. That is the law. Wolf taught me that. The memory of Wolf leaves my eyes stinging and my nose burning. I really do not expect to see Wolf again, despite my hopes.

I know none of this is likely to work. But I must try.

I pull out a spool of copper wires, flat scraps of metal—some scorched black, some half rusted—and an ancient handheld. I also have one of the rubies Raj found. I am going to need something else—part of a drone.

I put together the weapon Raj talked about—the laser. I work fast. For once, I do not need to remember. My fingers seem to know what to do without my needing to think. All too soon I have something that will work. But I need power.

I need an AT. I head to where they are kept. It takes what seems like a long time, but it is still night when I get there. With a silent apology to Bobcat, I take the AT she always rode. She will not need it now she is in the ground. I ride toward the Norm and back to the first platform where I met Skye. I hook up my device to the platform, connecting it so it will have power. It will probably pull a lot.

Now I need a drone to find me. I know how to make that happen. I have to be noticed. I throw rocks at the wall to the Norm. It takes two dozen rocks before I hear the hum. I sniff and tip my head back. The drone is coming down from the top of the wall. It must want to know what's banging on the Norm.

Crouching down, I lift my weapon. I have not tested it. It will either work or it won't. I point it at the drone and wait for the black ball to get closer. It puts out some kind of mechanical arm. I wait and take a breath. And press the button to the weapon. Nothing happens. I push the button again, glance down, see a loose wire and put my fingers on that.

The electrical charge knocks me back on my butt. I fall away and my weapon explodes. Metal flies. I duck. I hear the clatter of metal on metal and then a thud. Smoke tangs the air. Looking up, I see the drone on the ground, sputtering, sparks flying out. I get up, walk over and kick it. It goes silent. It really is nonfunctional. I glance at my weapon. It didn't work as planned, but it worked. I think I might have had too much power connected to it. I might have shorted out the platform, too.

Pulling out my knife, I start to take apart the drone. I have to work fast. The AI will send other drones.

The insides of the drones surprise me. It is partly organic, partly gear. Bits of data I have from the data orb start to make sense.

The data orb had a file called bioengineering. It was meant to increase the human lifespan but was adapted into military applications.

Drones.

And something else…into humans that were partly created. Cyborgs—that is the term the data orb used.

I realize why this data came to me. I am similar to the drone. I am part organic and part gear. I am descended from those cyborgs. I am not a Glitch. I'm something else. And I am going to make that work for me.

I pry the panels off the drone and get to the power source. I know this is an organic battery—one far more powerful than the old lithium ones Raj found in the Empties.

I pull out pieces I can use, weaving the circuitry of the drone into my jacket. The drone is quickly gutted. Inside, I find the lens I need. I pull that out and fashion an eyepiece. Now I just need a connect.

I glance at the platform. It is nonfunctional. But maybe I can use the drone.

I pull out the core and find the weapon the drone uses. It is more compact than the one I made. I hope it is functional still. I secure the drone's power source in my pouch and take the weapon and link it up to me. I walk over to the Norm's wall. I need a connect, and then I have to hack the door.

I touch the link and my palm closes over it. Tiny pinpricks dance over my skin. I blink.

Connection: Secure.

When I open my eyes I'm in the file room. I blink again to change it from cabinets to lines of light. They are much easier to work with. I glance around, searching for the right one. It shifts and vibrates over to hum in front of me. I pluck it with one finger. I pluck a dozen more so it will seem more like a general systems error. I do not want the AI to know what I am doing just yet.

I step back and out of the connect.

The door to the Norm is open. I glance inside. I want to make certain no Techs are around.

Just as the Outside is night right now, the Norm copies this pattern. The dome overhead is no longer sky blue, but it is dark. However, there are no stars, no points of light moving across the dome. It is just black. Lights near the ground mark paths to follow and more lights indicate doorways. Windows glow with shifting colors and I hear sounds from some of the buildings. It is as if the Techs are hearing stories being told to them. Maybe the AI tells stories the same way that Rogues do.

Stepping back into the Outside, I slip on the drone's visual and secure it with wire.

A virtual screen appears. I see both the Norm around me and lines of code. It takes a moment, and then the code shifts—or my brain does. The code becomes a language I know. I call up a map of the Norm and then overlay connections. Finally, I pull up a schematic of the AI's core systems—even a computer must live somewhere.

It is different than Raj said. The AI is not at the center of the Norm. She is below it and spread out across several systems. I call up additional information and trace down where the greatest power is located—that shows up at once.

I have a map now and some form of protection with the drone's weapon.

A soft hum carries to me on the wind. Turning, I see an AT heading toward me. It is coming in fast and I brace my legs wide. Who followed me? Is it Wolf?

The AT slows and stops and Raj steps off.

"What are you doing here?"

He glances at the doorway to the Norm and then to the smoking ruins of the drone, and finally back to me. His mouth pulls down but he shrugs. "I got up and saw your pouch was missing. You've been busy." He waves a hand to the parts of the drone I wear.

"I'm doing this alone."

His eyebrows lift high. "Really? And how are you doing that?"

I frown. I have the sudden urge to shoot him with the drone weapon, but I can't. I could hit him, however, and knock him on his ass.

He seems to know this for he drops his arms and says, "If we stand here arguing, that's just giving the AI time to track down your access. Or we could just get this done." He begins to walk past me, heading in the direction of the open doorway.

For a moment, I'm stunned and just stare at him. I make a frustrated noise, but I am also relieved to have help.

"I don't want this to be a repeat of last time." Catching up to him, I place my hand on his shoulder, forcing him to stop. He does and I stare into his eyes. "If I say bail, we do. This is dangerous, and I don't think the AI is going to give us another chance to walk away."

He brings up his hand and puts it over mine. His fingers are as cold as mine, but he gives my hand a squeeze. "You don't have to do this alone, Lib. I won't let you. We're going to fix the AI and the Norm."

I manage a small smile and nod. And I wish I had his certainty.

* * *

We step inside the Norm. The door stays open behind us. I might have broken it. Because it is night, it seems the Techs are asleep or inside. I nod the direction we need to take, and we head out at a slow jog.

"The core's not where you thought," I whisper to him.

He gives me a glance, but he follows me.

We stay in the shadows between buildings, half running. The drone's visual lays out the route we need to take. Raj's breathing becomes labored. Mine doesn't. I'm both faster and stronger.

Maybe it's all the training with Wolf—or maybe it's the bioengineering in me. The skills and power I used to get Raj out of the Norm return. They are stronger here. Or maybe it's just that I can access them here.

Either way, we're moving fast and I see the building we must enter. The doorway is dark. I nudge Raj. "Just up ahead!" I say, keeping my voice quiet.

I want to head straight to the AI core, but other blips appear on the visual. There is movement up ahead. Drones. I halt at the corner of the building, holding out an arm to stop Raj.

He leans against the wall. I watch for the drones. Two head down the screen, scanning, moving slowly. We stay still in the shadows. The drones slip past.

"How did you do that?" Raj mutters when he's caught his breath. He motions with his hand to the gear I'm wearing.

I bite my lip. But this isn't just about the gear. It's that I could integrate it with my systems.

"I'll explain later," I say quietly, hoping he'll drop it.

He puts a hand on my arm. "Drones are advanced biotech." He lets the words hang between us. His face is half cast in shadow making it difficult to know what he's thinking.

I shake my head and say, "We need to move now."

We dart out and run into the building. The Norm seems to think it needs to be daytime because the dome overhead is starting to lighten as if it is dawn. That doesn't matter. We head to the building indicated on the map. I yank on the door. It sticks, so I glance at the map and then at my hand. My palm tingles almost like a connect, except I remain in the Norm. To my surprise, the door swings open easily. We duck inside. Behind us, the door closes, leaving the room utterly black.

I find that I don't need light. My eyes adjust instantly, and the drone view shows everything in tints of green.

"I can't see anything!" Raj hisses.

"Don't worry. I can." I take his hand and lead him down a long hall.

According to the map, the AI core has to be housed below us. That's what's pulling the most power. Other systems are spread over the Norm, but Conie would need extra power. She has to be here. If we can reach her, we should be able to connect and hack her program. Then we can shut her down.

But it's not going to be that simple. Three drones appear on the map. They're small blips and they're heading our way. I glance around and heft the weapon in one hand. Can I make all three nonfunctional before they fire on us? I'm not sure I can and I fear it would only alert the AI to send more drones and Techs to swarm us.

I point ahead of us and then up.

Raj lets go of my hand and holds out his palm. “Need light and that,” he whispers and nods to the weapon in my hand. I give it to him and glance at the wall.

Light is not something my biotech was designed to need, but that doesn’t mean I can’t use it. Reaching out, I place my palm flat on the wall. Fibers tickle my skin. I concentrate and think one word. Lights!

The floors and ceiling brighten with that cool, blue light of the Norm.

Raj aims and fires the drone weapon. A beam of light that smells like burning metal shoots out. Raj sweeps the hall in front of us. I would have tried separate bolts, but his sweep does a better job. The light cuts the drones apart.

The drones crash to the floor and lay there, sparking, smoke rising from the remains.

I glance over at Raj. He’s breathing heavily and sweat gleams on his face. “How’d you know how to do that?”

He straightens and the corner of his mouth lifts. “Games when I was a kid. Before the AI kicked me out of the Norm.”

I nod. “This isn’t a game.”

Raj doesn't hand the weapon back, but he says, "Good. I'm not playing."

We start down the hall again. But there is no way Conie doesn't know we're here now.

Chapter Twenty-Eight

We find stairs and I follow them downward. And then it becomes a ladder to go even deeper. The map shows me this is repair access only. I wait for something to go wrong. Drones can't fit in the access tube, but my palms are damp and so is the back of my shirt. I was expecting more defenses, and I begin to think she is letting us walk in for her own reasons.

Glancing over at Raj, I see him lick the sweat off his upper lip. I wonder if he thinks the same thing I do, but I don't bother asking. It doesn't matter what we think.

The tube opens out into a narrow hallway. The drone visual shows we've almost reached the room we needed to access. The place is oddly quiet, except for a distant hum of power in electrical wires.

Raj glances over at me. "No drones?"

I shake my head. "I don't know what's next."

He shrugs. "Doesn't matter." He points to the door ahead. "That's the only way out for us."

We start down that hallway, our boots echoing against the metal floor. At the door, I stop and Raj stops a step behind me. I glance at the door. There is no way to open it. But a railing, just like the ones on the platforms in the Outside, rises up next to the door. It is thin and green. I reach for the railing and wrap my hand around it.

Instead of the prickle of a connect, a memory washes over me.

Muted blue walls, and the brighter white-blue lines of data. It's calming to watch it flow. I know she will protect me, watch over me as her favorite. I fret sometimes that I do not go into the Norm. But there is so much data to absorb. She shows me what is important.

The memory ends. It leaves me chilled to my core and my heart pounding. I glance over at Raj. He hasn't noticed a hesitation—meaning it happened in less than a nanosecond. He doesn't know. But I do.

I lived here. I was happy—or at least content.

He can't know that, I decide. Not ever.

"Are you going to open it or what?" Raj asks.

I glance at the railing, at my hand. I fear we are walking into a trap, but I cannot turn back.

I close my eyes. Whatever's beyond this door isn't going to be good. I vow I will do everything possible to make certain Raj makes it out of this alive.

With a steadying breath, I twist the railing and command the door to open. It does with a soft hiss like a breath.

Up to this point, it has all been so easy, so calm that I'm actually not expecting the swarm of things that fly at us. These aren't drones. They're scabs. I know what they are at once. Instead of being smooth globes like a drone, they have arms and legs and attachments sticking out of a flat disc. They rush at us. One catches my arm, its metal claw cutting my skin. Raj fires the drone weapon, slicing through metal. Another scab cuts into the copper wiring that interfaced with my drone visual. It goes dark. I drag it off and throw off the useless visual. Turning, I see Raj's jacket is torn. So are his pants. He fires again, slicing through a half dozen more scabs. More fall out of sliding panels that line the room.

Across from us is another doorway. This one is wide and open. "Raj, there," I shout the words and start for the doorway, ducking scabs, kicking at them, using every trick Wolf ever taught me. My hands sting from striking out at metal. I hear the power hum on the drone weapon Raj carries.

Glancing back, I see he hasn't moved. He waves me ahead. "Go," he shouts.

I call out his name, but a scab slams into me, sending me flying through the doorway. The door slides shut. Getting up, I pound on it and my fists dent the metal. "Raj!"

Stepping back, I look for the railing to connect and open the door, but a soft voice stops me.

"Welcome home, Lib."

My skin prickles and my blood seems to freeze. That voice echoes inside my head and the ache lifts inside my chest.

I've missed you.

The words whisper in the back of my mind. I shove them aside and turn.

There is nothing to miss. I no longer belong here. I do not miss Conie!

Conie forms her projection in front of me. It starts with an outline, and then scan lines fill in the hair, the face, the eyes, and the mouth. She assembles from the top down. She wears a tunic of cloth today, like the one I had on when I woke in the Outside. Her lips are almost smiling, and her eyes are almost welcoming. But they are the wrong color. They are an impossible electric blue.

"You've done a good job, Lib."

"Getting here? Did you think a couple of drones would stop me?"

She takes steps toward me, one hand outstretched as if she could touch me. She needn't bother with this, and I wonder why she does. "Of course not. Their purpose was to take out the glitched Tech with you, but the scabs can do that."

"You wanted me here?" It's not really a question. I can still hear the noise of the drone weapon on the other side of the door, whining and high. I walk through Conie and head for the opposite side of the room, where the controls must exist.

I have to stop in front of the controls. There are so many railings and status lights.

I have to get into the system, but how?

Conie walks over to my side. Her feet do not quite meet the floor and she makes no sounds when she walks. But she smiles at me. "I knew you would return." Her voice is calm and might be sweet if it wasn't so cold. "You were meant to return once you fulfilled your purpose." She struggles with a frown. It doesn't quite form and she gives up and says, "You were meant to come alone. Why did you bring a glitched Tech?"

I study the controls in front of me, but I ask her, "Why not? And what do you mean I was 'meant to'?"

The projection flickers but remains still. "The purpose I gave you. It is your entire meaning. It is the reason you exist."

I have to look at her, even though she is not really there. "Reason…" I trail off because I know this is the truth.

I am a created being—manufactured. I…no…I have a mother. I have Conie. Images blur in my mind. I have a mother, and yet…I don't. How can both be true? Conie wears my mother's face. I know this for a fact. And yet, I also know I've been engineered. Given purpose by the AI—and then manipulated by Conie.

I stiffen my back and stare at Conie. There is no going back now—and there's no stopping Conie from telling me the truth.

I reach for the control railing. But a sharp prick stabs my lower back. It's like a connect, but different. I glance around. A glowing cable extends from me. It's buried in my lower back. I know this at once. The data dump rips information from my skull. With a cry, I fall to my knees and clutch my head. Memories are dragged from me—new ones, old ones. They try to come together only to twist apart.

Conie steps up to me. "Sending the glitched Techs wasn't a good solution. I did not anticipate they would join up with the decedents of those who rejected the security of the Norm." She strokes my head with a hand as if I can feel her touch. I struggle to fight the download, but I can't. What will I be without memories? Will I be back to being nothing? Empty as the ruined cities? "The program was sound—recycle glitched Techs to the Outside. Instead, they did not recycle. They return and connect through back doors and use low-level systems to steal. Stealing is wrong, Lib. Bad enough that this affects the Norm, but it puts schedules in danger. That puts everything inside the Norm at risk. I protect the Norm. I keep it functional. I maintain the schedule for the plan that will save humanity. The departure is exact and cannot be delayed."

I choke out a cry and flail at the connect to my spine. I can't reach it.

"That is why I grew you. The perfect Glitch to be put in the Outside. Your purpose was to find the other Glitches. Search them out and return with the data on their location. The drones terminate too few and too randomly. This calls for a large-scale extinction of all threats to the Norm."

"No." I choke out the word. Is this true? The drone attacks were random. I am not at fault for that. But I am now.

Conie straightens. "You have given me the location. I will correct the error. Imperfection constantly burdens humanity, but that can be remedied. In the end, the survival of humanity is all that matters."

The download takes locations and landmarks but skips past Bear's choice to go back into ground and the sorrow I felt. It starts to download Wolf's image and skips again. It can't deal with emotion. That is Conie's flaw. She has no physical body She can simulate feeling, but she can't understand it. That's why she needed me, and that's what I can use against her.

I think about Wolf—about how his body pressing against me left me tingling and warm. I think of his mouth covering mine, how he stole my breath. I focus on the pride of getting a hit in on Wolf and the pleasure of his smile.

Conie tips her head to one side. "What are you doing, Lib?"

"Something you can't," I tell her. I let the tears spring to my eyes. I think of Raj, fighting for his life and how it felt to have him put his hand over mine. I think of Bird's fear and anger, my frustration, and I let go of a low growl. The download stutters again, and I use that instant and flip it around. I start to pull at the data. I drag back my memories and then start shifting through Conie's to find more.

"Lib?" Conie's projection flickers. "You cannot. You have no access."

"You just gave it to me." I struggle to my feet. I'm searching through terabytes and terabytes, more data than I can process, so I simply grab and go for more. I hit older data—it's structured differently and I begin to pull at that, following twined threads.

Conie flickers again as if she cannot maintain the projection with me in the data stream. Her eyes shine even brighter. "You will set the program back. This cannot be allowed."

"So stop me." I throw the words at her. I also throw more emotions—love, fear, joy, terror—into the data stream. She blinks twice. The cable snaps away from me and snakes back into the control panel.

Staggering, I put a hand to my lower back. I feel the blood oozing warm from my skin. I turn to try and access the control panel, but behind me, I hear the hiss of the door. Glancing at the doorway, I see scabs pour into the room, their metal gleaming and appendages clattering.

Conie disappears, but her voice remains. "Lib is no longer functioning within parameters of the program. Terminate."

Cables snake out from the controls. I jump back and dodge them. Wolf's training has become instinct. One dives at my neck. Pain tears through me, making me grit my teeth. This time, the cable is simply out to pull the life from me.

Reaching up, I grab hold of the cable and yank hard. The end comes away bloody and sparking. With a growl, I use the cable to knock the scabs out of my way.

"Attempting reboot of Lib program," Conie says, her voice calm.

"I'm not a program. Growth is life, you said. Well, I've grown. So get used to it."

I turn to the doorway, but Raj is down and struggling to reach the far doorway and the railing there. And too many scabs swarm the room. I need to connect—to shut them down and find us a way out.

But going in may give Conie the perfect opportunity to get what she needs—me dead.

Or maybe it'll end with her dead.

I slap a hand on the railing next to the door. Pricks sting my palm, and I blink.

Connection: Secure.

Chapter Twenty-Nine

I'm inside, but this artificial world is not right. The same cool blue washes the room, but smoke hazes it, too. What sounds like metal crashing echoes from all sides. Did I do this with the download connect and the data I pulled from the AI, or is something else happening?

Sentinels form at once and come at me. Black and skeletal, they appear to be made of metal that is almost liquid. They have arms and legs but no head or face. They don't need faces. They only mimic humanity.

One sentinel reaches for me, but I dodge out of its grasp. With a blink, I'm in another part of the data stream. The sentinels follow. I head in the direction the smoke seems to be coming from. I need to call up the lines to shut down the scabs and drones—if I can get a breath long enough to do that.

The sentinels follow me. I blink again and end up in the room with cabinets. Looking up, I see Raj on a tall ladder. Somehow, he made a connect and got in here, but I don't know what he's doing. He moves three times normal speed, faster than he'd ever be able to move in reality, and I remember he was raised to work within this world of data streams and information. Sentinels seem to form out of nothing, hover around Raj, and shoot out electricity from their hands.

Just like with Skye when I first found her in the connect.

I am tired of these sentinels. This time I don't wait to call up the lines of light. I let loose my anger and spread out my hands. Light flows from my fingertips in bolts that vaporize the sentinels. Raj leans back to avoid a bolt. He falls and I catch him before he hits the floor. He slams into my arms, taking us both to the floor, which dissolves and ends with us in an empty, blue-tinged room. Raj grabs my arm. "Lib, did you do it?"

I shake my head. "No, things have changed."

A whip of energy comes at us, ripping between us so Raj is forced to release me. Looking up, I see a sentinel. I stretch out my hand and don't even bother with energy. I simply close my fist and the sentinel crumples into dust. The download has left me able to control this world, but the AI will be trying to change that.

I grab Raj's hand and blink again. We end in a room that looks as if it is the Outside. I realize it is a room created by my memories that were downloaded. With a wave of my hand, I wipe it away and delete it. Raj stares at me. "You failed?" Anger is tight in his voice, but beneath that, I hear the heartbreak. Until this moment, I didn't realize how deeply he wanted this to work.

I shake my head. "More like I never got the chance. But, Raj, listen, there's no way to fix the AI. I saw it in…" I run out of words there. How do I tell Raj I've been in the AI's core data stream and yet couldn't do anything to stop her?

“Raj, the AI isn’t just an artificial intelligence with the capacity to learn and grow. Conie is a digital composite of a person. When I…I hacked the system, I found the original brain patterns and personality imprints. Conie’s a construct based on her creator. And the AI’s creator pushed her being into Conie, but something went wrong.”

Raj is staring at me. “What does that mean for us? It’s not a computer? Not a program or system?”

“It’s evolved far beyond that. It’s fully realized and it’s going to fight any attempt to make it change or put it back in a box.”

He stares at me, his face set in grim lines. Both of us know that if the AI can’t be fixed, we will likely die here or in the Norm.

“Then let’s get out of here,” Raj says in a low tone.

“There’s more,” I whisper. I clench my eyes shut. It’s not my fault the others died from the drones who found them, but it will be my fault if more die. The AI still has some of my memories in the download. I open my eyes and say, “The Rogues are in trouble. The AI knows where they are. They have to move or they’ll be massacred. Skye, too.”

A slash of energy falls on us. I stand and face the sentinel. It’s a stupid thing with a simple program. I slap it into oblivion. But what I really want to do is delete the core program that keeps creating the sentinels. When the sentinel is gone, Raj stands and gives me a look, but he takes my hand when I offer it to him.

I blink. We end up in a room made of nothing but lines of light. Raj spins and falls. I glance at him and see he has closed his eyes and is sweating. The room is disorienting to him so I put in a floor and give him a hand up. "It's okay now."

He opens his eyes and faces me. "How are you doing all this?"

I shrug. "Let's just call this built-in ability." I start to pluck at the lines, searching for ideas. The AI has shielded the drone and sentinel programs—the scabs, too. I can't access any of them without taking time to undo her locks. I need another way out.

A screech sounds behind me, and I glance back to see Raj hit by a bolt from a sentinel. They've followed us here and I thought they couldn't. Raj hits the floor I put in, electricity encircling his ankle, tearing into him until his entire body convulses. He screeches in pain. I start for him, ready to help, just like I did with Skye, but he yells at me, "No. Go! Save the Rogues. Save yourself!"

"Like that's going to happen." I flatten the sentinel with a wave and drag Raj to his feet. He sways there, shaking, his face pale. "We can both get out of here."

He shakes his head. "You need a distraction."

"No, I need an idea. I need lightning at my fingertips and the wind at my back, and…and here comes trouble." More sentinels appear. I grab Raj's hand and blink. We end back in the room with file cabinets. We're losing time, but I have no idea how much time has passed in reality.

Conie is distracting us—meaning she may already have sent out drones to hunt down the Tracker clan. If Conie makes this plan work, she'll go after other Rogues and the rest of the Glitches. She will find Skye and kill her. She will find Wolf. A sharp pain contracts in my chest. I have to stop the AI.

I glance at Raj. "You're right. We need a distraction."

He holds out his hand. "Give me a weapon to do what you do to the sentinels. I'll watch your back."

It's a good idea. I manufacture a weapon like the drones have in the real world. This will work in this artificial construct to tear apart the sentinels. I tell Raj, "It works just like anywhere—point and press the button."

He nods. I turn away and summon the lights back. I hope Raj is not going to end up sacrificing himself for me, but we might both end up sacrificing our lives for the others.

That idea settles into me, and suddenly this is not a bad thing. To know others will go on if I do not. I understand the clan now. I know what they mean when they say the clan must come first. I have fought that idea, but now I see it as a good thing—to give so that others can live. For the first time, I understand Bear's choice. He didn't want the clan to be in danger because of him.

Well, it is because of me.

I find a line of light that connects me to drone visuals. I pull in a sharp breath. The drones fly high above dry ground. They are already on their way. I'm too late.

I search the lines of light looking for some other way to stop the drones.

There must be something!

There is no failsafe and no code to recall them. Conie knew I would try to stop her and has removed the means of anyone stopping this. Frustrated, I slam a palm on the lines of light, making them all vibrate and cry out.

I want lighting at my fingertips.

The lines sway and shift, and one forms in front of me.

Access: Storm.

A jumble of information pours out on how to create a storm. A severe storm. The AI can create them or use them to make rain—or to hold back the rain. The AI is starving this world. She is making it barren.

I don't finish that train of thought because I can use this storm to destroy, too. Didn't Bird say I would bring destruction with me? I will now.

I pull up the light, pluck it and put in the code to create one of the biggest storms in history. In my mind's eye, I can see it swirling in, the sand blinding and hitting the drones, finding the crevices in their electronics and filling them with sand.

I picture the drones getting swallowed by sand. Then rain will hit and short out the electronics and the wind will dash them into the hillsides until they explode and nothing is left but scrap.

This will work. This will stop them.

When my storm is hatched, I let the lines of light fade way. Now I can get Raj and me out of here. The storm will hit the Norm as well, and the AI will be too busy dealing with protecting the Norm to bother with us.

But when I turn to see Raj, he's gone.

Chapter Thirty

I end the connect and stagger. The real world now seems unreal. I have to shake my head and blink several times before I remember to really breathe. Raj has to be here in the other room, still connected. The AI is no longer here and the control room is dark. Conie has moved, I know. She shifted to another location to secure herself.

Stumbling through the open doorway, I hope to find Raj in the other room. But it's empty. Black scars from the drone weapons cover the walls, but there isn't so much as a scrap of metal from any of the scabs Raj destroyed.

Maybe he escaped already and he's waiting for me outside?

But how could he have done that?

I'm not sure what happened to Raj, but I have to get out before the storm passes and Conie has time to come looking for me. I head down the hall and up the ladder and then up the stairs and out of the building. I'm running and out of breath.

In the Norm, I pause. The Techs seem to be inside buildings, even though the dome shows daylight. I can hear the storm pounding at the dome, rattling it slightly. For the first time, I wonder if the Rogues will survive the storm. It's too much like my dream of the tunnels filling. I will never forgive myself if I have made that dream come true.

I start down the path that I used to get to the building.

Drones come at me, weapons armed, and it's obvious they have been programmed to kill.

Conie must be angry.

For some reason, that leaves me smiling.

I don't have the powers I have inside the virtual world where I can smash sentinels with a thought. Here I dodge the beams from the drone weapons and wince if one burns too close and tears through the cloth or singes my hair. The beams leave a stink in the air, but I follow the smell of rain—of the Outside.

The door is still stuck open.

One drone hovers low and close. I jump up and smash my fist into it. It falters and falls. My hand stings. But I jump on the drone, smash the edge of the control panel, and yank it open to rip out its weapon. Now it's almost a fair fight.

I use the weapon like Raj did—sweeping it across the sky and across buildings. The weapon singes the dome and suddenly the drones shift, heading to the dome. Rain and wind leak in through the scar I made. The drones seem frantic to make repairs, and now their weapons become like torches that can mend the rip I made.

That gives me the time I need. I sprint for the door. Behind me, I hear the whine of a drone. Heat tears into my back. I cry out, but I still don't stop running.

I race through the Norm, weaving between buildings, dodging under trees. I wish I had the drone viewer with the map, but I have to hope my memory of the path is still good. Straight, left, right, right.

I have to keep correcting my course because Techs begin to walk out of the buildings, their expressions blank.

I slam into a man three times my size. He wears the same white cloth as everyone else in the Norm, but his expression is empty. He reaches for me with a beefy hand and grabs the collar of my shirt, jerking me up off my feet. I try to wiggle out of his grasp and slap at his hands.

His other hand comes up too and closes around my throat. He squeezes. Air catches in my throat and lodges in my chest. I kick and cough.

Remembering my training with Wolf, I raise up my arms together, pushing them between the man's massive forearms. Black spots form at the edges of my vision. I bring my arms down, folding them out so that my elbows catch the crook of his arms. His arms buckle and he lets go of me.

My feet hit the ground. I pull in wheezing breaths of delicious air as I crouch low and duck away before he reaches for me again.

He catches me by the ankle and jerks me back. I turn and bring my other leg up and around, aiming a fast, hard kick to his face. Something crunches beneath my boot. Blood splatters across his face. He staggers back, letting go of me.

Twisting around again, I scramble to my feet and run. I run as though my life depends on it because it does. Behind me, I hear more Techs coming after me.

Ahead, I can see the storm raging through the door that is stuck open. Sand swirls, so dense that you cannot see through it. The wind bites into the dome. Drones hover over the door—trying to repair it and close it. The storm is a beast in the sky, waiting to devour me. I glance over my shoulder at the approaching Techs and know that if they get hold of me, I'm lost. Conie will never let me go.

Running for the doorway, I pull a ragged strip of cloth from the pouch bouncing at my side and cover my face and head as best I can.

The door starts to slip closed. I lunge forward, throwing myself into the Outside, half falling and half sliding. The door catches the heel of my boot, and then sneaks closed, leaving me to face the storm I created.

Chapter Thirty-One

I'm going to die. As soon as I step into the storm, the wind slaps at me. It howls so loudly it deafens me. The sand scratches at my eyes and scours my skin. It catches in my throat, forcing its way down. I put an arm over my face to try and keep the cloth over my head, but I can't see much. The door behind me is closed and there is no way forward.

I'm going to die here and now, alone.

Raj is not waiting for me. I don't know where he is now. How can he be back in the Norm—or even in a connect? I have no idea where he vanished to, but now I think maybe he has the kinder fate.

I collapse in a heap. Sand sweeps up around me, half burying me. I think I hear my name being called, but I am certain it is just something I wish would happen. Another yell carries to me with the howl of the wind.

"Here!"

It sounds like Wolf, but he can't be here. He is hiding in the tunnels, fighting not to be buried by my storm.

I slump against the wall to the Norm, ready to be buried. Giving up seems a good idea right now. I saved the Tracker clan. I found the Glitches. And it's not my fault anyone died.

Sometimes that just happens. But I am ready to go back into the ground. I see Bear take the knife from Wolf and I smile. It is a good choice to give up so others can go on. Bobcat would do the same, and I am Tracker clan. The law is clan comes first.

Strong arms scoop me up. It is nice to be held. I snuggle closer to a man's chest, hard and muscled. For an instant, it seems like being back in a connect-reality and nonreality blur. But I can hear Wolf's heartbeat. I smell his scent. The virtual world only lets you see illusion. It doesn't do a very good job with all the senses. Prying my eyes open, I squint up. Wolf wears cloth over his face, and it almost hides his eyes. But I know this is Wolf. Only he has that scent like dry sage.

He's come to save me.

Vaguely, I see the AT parked nearby. It is one of the bigger ones. It also has cloth over the cage now, but the wind tries to strip it away. Wolf carries me to the AT. The engine hums to life. Beside him at the controls sits Bird. She glances at me and frowns and I think I hear her say something about destruction. But she has a cloth over her head and face too. The AT turns and ploughs a path away from the Norm. The wind pushes at us as if it's trying to tip us over. I can't see much, but something wet stings my face.

I hold out a hand. Another drop of water falls from the sky. I smile. "About time my rain showed up. Going to be a wet one, Wolf. Hope the tunnels are ready."

Then I give up holding on and let the world fade into nothing.

*　　　*　　　*

I wake to see Croc bending over me. He straightens. "Can you sit?"

I nod, but when I try I find I can only lift a hand. Croc takes it and pulls me upright. The world spins. Coming around behind me, Croc spreads something cool over my back. It's then I realize I don't have a shirt on. "Never seen burns this bad on someone still alive."

"That's nice." I frown. "Did you give me something?"

Croc waves something burning and smoking under my nose. It smells…nice. "Just a little smoke to relax you. Didn't know how you'd wake. Any headache? Dizziness? Do you want to throw up?"

I frown. "If I say yes to any of that, I'm not getting out of here." Croc comes back around, his fingers shiny from the stuff he put on my back. It has a smell like a plant. He puts the jar of stuff down and hands me a shirt. It has a burn hole in the back. He glances at it, tosses it away and hands me a shirt made from animal skin.

I take it and put it on, glad it's soft. Every muscle in my body screams, but the smoke at least makes the screams seem like they come from a long way away. “Let me guess—council still wants to see me?”

“More like everyone.” Croc folds his arms over his chest. “I hear a tale you came in with Wolf and Bird and a storm that’s filled our drink storage. Won’t need to do a connect for some time is what I hear. I also hear there’s drones littered across the land like some big old wind came along and smashed them into the hillsides. Going to be parts for gear for a time.”

I nod. I also manage to get onto my feet. Croc lets me, watching me the whole time. “If you’re good enough to stand, best go face the others. It’ll get Wolf to stop poking his face in here every five minutes.”

With a smile for him, I head for the main room. I have to trail my fingers along one wall of the tunnels to stay on my feet. I am dizzy, my head aches, and my stomach keeps twisting on me as if it’s about to rebel. But I manage to step into the main room.

Everyone stops talking and heads swivel so their stares land on me. I don’t really care. I’ve faced the AI and my own past and I’m not sure anything can hurt me anymore.

Wolf stands and comes over to me. He puts a hand on my waist as if he’s going to catch me if I fall. And I might.

“You’re hurt.”

“Not that bad or Croc wouldn’t have let me out.”

He gives a nod and turns to help me to the fire, but Lion blocks the way. "Why is she back?"

I glance at him, eyes narrowed. Lion meets my stare, but then his gaze drops and he backs down. I push Wolf's hand away and stride over to where the Rogues sit. Skye is by herself, and that breaks something inside me.

I stride over to Skye, grab her hand, pull her to her feet and bring her into the circle of Rogues near the fire. Someone starts muttering. I glance around at the faces turned up to me.

"Shut it and listen." I plunk Skye down next to me. "We don't have time to be stupid. And the differences we have are going to make a difference in our lives. Now, you want to blame me for everything that has happened—well, you aren't entirely wrong to do so. It's a long story, mine is, and I'll tell it on a long night, but right now I've got important things to say. You want to hear them or you want to slap your hands over your ears and close your eyes and act like a mole that doesn't like the light?"

Mole ducks her head, but not before I see her cheeks flame red. I glance around. The Rogues all swap glances. I start to see bodies stir, but Bird steps up. "You best hear her. She brought the storm—the destruction. You'd best listen."

I swap a stare with Bird. I'm not sure we'll ever be friends, but I can respect her honesty. It's time for some of my own. I look back at the Rogues, and I take a breath and a last glance at Wolf for courage. Skye touches my leg. I glance at her and she smiles up at me and gives me a nod.

I look around again at the group. I have to make them understand.

"First off—I'm not a Glitch. We'll I am and I'm not. I was never a Tech. I was made to be what I am and you'll have to take that as it is."

"We're all made what we are," Elk says.

I flash her a smile. It's not exactly support, but it's close enough. "I've been into the Norm—Raj and I went there to try and fix the AI. But we can't. It's not fixable. It's also not what I thought it was. We hacked the system, and the AI tried to download what I know. The AI was sending drones here, and the AI will try that again, so we'll have to leave."

"But I like it here," Mouse says. She glances around and frowns. "I do."

"We'll have to move, but there's worse. The AI—I've seen her plans. Her program."

"Her?" Mole sits straighter.

"The AI has a name—Conie. Its letters put together from other words, but it's a name. The AI also isn't happy with things as they are. The AI doesn't just want everything. She wants to leave. She wants to take the Norm to another world. The program is to start humanity over on fresh earth. I'm not sure the AI can find it, but that doesn't matter. What does matter is that the AI wants all Glitches and Rogues terminated. The AI is coming. So is a war with her."

Mutters spread across the group. Mouse looks up and asks, "Why should we trust you?"

"Because I've seen her plans. I've been in her code, meaning in her head. She tried to download me, but I got a lot from her in the process. She's coming for us. We need to be ready to fight her if we want to live."

The Rogues start to mutter and then talk, some waving away my words, others telling those who don't believe they'd best listen. A wave of exhaustion washes over me. My knees start to buckle. I have nothing else to share with them.

I start to slide down, and Wolf's arm wraps around me, keeping me upright. He pulls me close and I tell him, "I need to talk to you."

With a nod he looks at the Rogues, his voice lifts up loud and clear. "You all know law. Lib brought us water. Lib brings news now. Bird has spoken for Lib. Lib stays unless anyone wants to say differently." He glances around the group.

Lion mutters something, but no one else does, and a few gazes slide away from Wolf. Wolf gives a nod. He lifts me up even though I protest and carries me over to where the Glitches sit. “Really? Here?”

“We can talk.” He frowns at me and touches a finger to my cheek. I wince, so there must be a bruise there. “You should see Croc again,” Wolf whispers. He presses his mouth to the corner of my mouth.

My heart quickens, but I shake my head. “There’s something more important.”

His eyebrows rise high. I’m reminded of Raj, but I can’t think about that right now. I swallow hard, and Wolf says, “A war?”

“The AI—she’s more than a computer or a system. I’m afraid, too, she might be able to learn to hate. She doesn’t understand emotion, but she can learn.” I bite down on the words about how the AI created me. I can’t bring myself to mention my origins, not yet. I’d like to believe Wolf of all people would understand, but I’m not sure I can expect that from anyone. And I need him to believe the rest of what I have to say.

“I don’t know what happened to Raj.” My nose stings and I wipe at it. “I left him. I didn’t search.”

Wolf rubs a hand over my shoulders. “You did what you had to do. I know you, Lib. You didn’t even want to leave Bear when he asked it.”

I sniffle. "I know… but I still can't make myself feel better about it. But the AI. She isn't just hoarding resources. She has a program—a plan. The AI is out to save humanity—I don't know from what. But the Norm isn't just a dome. It's a huge circle. It goes a huge distance underground, and the AI is turning the Norm into…into something that could leave this world. It's like a…an ark, it's called. A ship that can go from this planet and travel through the distance to another star and another world. She intends to take the Techs with her. And she's got a schedule. The AI is going to strip this world until there's nothing left. And then she'll go."

Wolf frowns but lifts a shoulder. "So let the Norm go. No more AI could be good. No more drones. No more trouble."

I grab Wolf's hand. "No more world. The Norm is huge. For it to leave, it's going to tear this world apart. And the AI is not about to let anyone or anything get in the way of the schedule for leaving."

Wolf's jaw hardens. He looks down. When he looks up, I see understanding in his eyes. Voice low, he says, "When she leaves, we're dead. Then we have to keep the AI from going. Simple, right?" He touches my cheek again.

I want to laugh. Simple—right. And impossible. But the Rogues face tough odds every day. And they survive.

*   *   *

I stand at the edge of the tunnels, staring out at the vast distances of the Outside. The mountains I know are now the Empties. And far away—but not too far—is the Norm. The Outside, dangerous as it is, is my home. I'm ready to fight for it. Not that long ago such a thought would have scared me. It might have left me quivering, frightened.

I'm not afraid. I've been through bad things and come out.

And I'm not alone in this battle.

Wolf comes up from the tunnels to stand with me. He slings his arm across my shoulders, pulling me close. My own arm goes to his waist, my hand lingering on his hips. He presses his lips to my forehead—a kiss he calls it. That is something the AI doesn't understand. The AI will never understand touch. The AI will forever be alone—and will not understand just what that means. I could almost pity the AI if she didn't want to destroy everything just to save something that I'm not sure really exists.

But those are worries for another day. The storm left the air smelling sweet and the ground damp. Plants push up—grass as green as in the Norm. I hear the croak of animals that Wolf calls frogs. In the distance, the wolves sing and Wolf throws back his head and howls with them.

I grin up at him.

The council met tonight. Skye is to choose if she wishes to be a Tracker. I got to be the one to tell her and her face lit up, bright as the sun. She is to visit the Empties and come back a Tracker. For the first time ever, we are not Rogues and Glitches. We are clan.

Together, we will face whatever comes next.

When war comes, we will survive.

This I vow tonight to Wolf.

End of 'The Glitch'

The Glitches Series Book One

Book Two of The Glitches series, **The Empties,** is out NOW!

Keep reading for an exclusive extract.

Thank you!

Sign up to Ramona Finn's mailing list to be notified of new releases and get exclusive excerpts!

Sign Up at http://www.subscribepage.com/i9w7w9

You can also find me on Facebook!

www.facebook.com/ramonafinnbooks/

Sneak Peek

The Empties

The Glitches Book Two

Blurb

Is survival worth any price?

Cast out of the Norm, Lib must fight for every second of life among the Rogues in the desert wasteland that is now her home, scavenging in abandoned cities known as the Empties. With the help of fellow Glitch Skye she hopes to hack the AI that will allow them to return to the city and save her family. There's just one problem: Lib's memories are missing.

Lib isn't like other Glitches. Her ability to merge with technology is causing a rift in her newfound family, and putting them in danger. Soon she'll have to choose whether to return to the Norm or stay with the people she's come to rely on in the Outside. When her desire to know the truth about herself forces her to return to the Norm, handsome Rogue leader Wolf Tracker insists on accompanying her to the lion's den.

There, she meets an old friend—but Lib is no longer sure they can be trusted. When she learns a horrifying truth about the AI and her mother's part in it, Lib is shaken to the core. Now, she'll have to decide if humanity's survival is worth a bloody cost.

Get The Empties at http://amzn.to/2mglEns

The Empties
The Glitches Book Two

Extract

The hot air hits me in quick blasts that pick up my short hair, slapping it against my forehead and the edges of my face. I keep running. The breeze is almost enough to cool the sweat that's collected at the base of my neck and where the biogear connects to me through my skin. The tiny screen above my left eye flashes a warning. Drones fly close behind me—right where I want them. I push myself to run faster, legs pounding, breaths short and fast. The biogear makes it possible. Still, my body burns with the effort.

I don't bother to glance behind and confirm what the biogear is telling me. The drones, sent out by the AI…by Conie…hum with a soft whine. I feel no fear as I might have once when facing the machines the AI uses to try and spy on us. I am no longer scared. This is a war. One I'm determined we will win. The AI intends to leave our world—and leave nothing behind. We fight now for survival—but we need to know more about the AI. Just as she tries to know about how we intend to stop her.

And we will stop her. We must.

I can't help the surge of adrenaline that pushes me to run even faster, despite the ache starting in my left calf.

I can do this.

This is the first real trial of the biogear—gear we take from drones both old and new, ones we take down with rocks and whatever else will pull them from the sky. We take the gear and adapt it to work with our bodies. The AI once wiped my memories—but not all of them. And I know more about gear than any other Glitch ever has. Just as I know the black drones have no intelligence—the AI does not share her power. But they have gear—and we can use that to make us faster, able to see more and fight them.

I spare a glance around me—a fast scan. The canyon narrows ahead of me. Relief swells within me. I'm close. All I have to do is push a little harder and get the drones into the trap.

Studying the biogear screen, I pick out the drone that is closest. It's black, the body dusty and has not extended any arms. It is ahead of three others.

Perfect.

The biogear wraps around my back, arms extend down from it to my legs, helping me move more fluidly, letting me do more with less effort. I change direction. Instead of going into the narrowing mouth of the canyon, I head straight for one of the towering rock walls.

Behind me, the whine of the drone grows louder.

With a jump and a spin, I slam my boots into the rock wall. Small shards tumble out from beneath my feet. I push off of the wall and into the air, tucking so my feet spin over my head and I fly over the drone.

The drone is too slow to correct. It starts a turn but smashes into the rock with an explosion of black from its shell. It gives a louder whine and falls to the dust. Now we have more parts to build more biogear.

I twirl and hit the ground, landing with a jarring thud and in a low crouch that lets me face the remaining three drones. They seem almost like black shadows against the hard blue of the sky—like birds without wings, or clouds that have no softness.

Turning, I start a sprint down the narrow canyon.

The biogear lets me run longer and harder, but my side aches now. Each breath seems harder. My throat is dry. But I have to do this.

We need to know more about what the AI plans—we need the drones to connect to the AI mainframe.

And this may be the only way I ever find out what happened to Raj.

82365705R00177

Made in the USA
San Bernardino, CA
14 July 2018